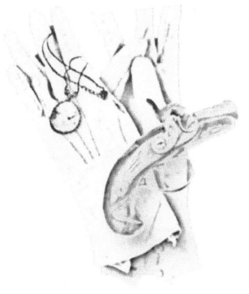

An Agent for Darcy

The Pinkerton Matchmaking Series
Book #17

By:

Laura Beers

Even though this book is a work of fiction, the Pinkerton Agents and their exploits are very real.

Allan Pinkerton, a Scottish immigrant, and Edward Rucker, a Chicago attorney, started the North-Western Police Agency in the early 1850s. It later became the Pinkerton Detective Agency.

Established in the U.S. by Allan Pinkerton in 1855, the Pinkerton National Detective Agency was a private security guard and detective agency. Pinkerton agents were hired as both bodyguards and detectives by corporations and individuals. They were active in stopping strikes, illegal operations, guarding train shipments, and searching for Western outlaws such as the James and Younger gangs.

Pinkerton agents were known to be tough yet honest. For the most part, they followed local and state laws. However, as with most situations, a few were known to be ruthless. Local law didn't always approve of having an agent in town since they could investigate more fully than the sheriff. Going undercover gave the agents greater leeway for investigations but could also lead to corruption and violence.

As the West became more settled, crime increased, and local authorities were at times overwhelmed. It was not uncommon for Pinkerton agents to be hired to track down the worst of these criminals. Not encumbered by state or local boundaries, the agents followed and pursued their quarry where the clues led them.

The Pinkerton Agency was also one of the first companies to hire women. Kate Warne led the way for the women agents that followed her.

As the case load grew, new offices were established around the country, with the main office in Chicago, Illinois.

We created this series with these heroic men and women in mind. These are works of our imagination and no way reflect the true cases or activities that the Pinkerton Agency may have engaged in.

These are our stories of the men and women that braved danger and love to bring their own brand of justice.

Allan Pinkerton's agents were required to comply with a specific code of conduct while working for the Pinkerton Detective Agency.

According to the agency's records, agents were to have no addiction to "drinking, smoking, card playing, low dives or slang".

Additionally, a Pinkerton agent …

- Could not accept bribes
- May never compromise with criminals
- Should willingly partner with local law enforcement
- Must refuse divorce cases or those initiating scandal
- Would be expected to turn down reward money
- Cannot raise fees without client's prior knowledge
- Should keep clients appraised on an on-going basis

Sat. April 22, 1871

Female Agents to join National Detective Agency.

Help Wanted: female agents to join the National Pinkerton Detective Agency

Seven years ago, the National Pinkerton Detective Agency moved into the new office location at 427 Chain Bridge Road, Denver, Colorado Territory. Since then stories have swirled of brave men solving crimes and fighting for justice.

But a new time has evolved, and the agency is now seeking able-bodied women to join the ranks of private investigations.

We need daring women who seek adventure and are of sound mind and body. You will help the criminal elements answer for their crimes and secure safety for their victims.

You will train with an existing agent, and after your first case, you will earn the rank of private detective. Paid training, transportation, uniforms, and accommodations will be provided. You will become a part of a noble profession and pave the way into the future.

This editorial has been placed in newspapers throughout the nation, so the quickest responses are appreciated.

Please send inquiries and a list of skills to Mr. A. Gordon at the above noted address. Interviews will occur on the premises the week of May 16, 1871.

Ed.

Chapter 1

Darcy Spencer could not abide marriage proposals. Over the past six months, she had grown to loathe them. Good ones, bad ones, they were all the same… unwanted.

Standing with her back to the railing of her front porch, Darcy attempted to be cordial as Pastor Whitaker blundered through his offer. Oh, he was an attractive man with dark, wavy hair and broad shoulders, but she cared little for appearances. She had been fooled once by her late husband and his boyish charms.

Pastor Whitaker stopped speaking, and his hopeful gaze pleaded with her to take a chance on him. "What do you think, Mrs. Spencer?"

Darcy gave him a sympathetic smile as she observed him wringing the hat in his hands. Poor man had even worn his best suit to mark the special occasion. "Pastor Whitaker, I thank you for the honor that you have bestowed upon me, but I am not interested in marrying again."

Instead of leaving in a huff, or pleading his case, as the other men had done, Pastor Whitaker gave her an understanding nod. "Josh hurt you real bad, but not all men are like him. There are good, honorable men in this town that would treat you right." He gave her a knowing look and finished, "That is if you'd give one of them a chance."

She appreciated his straightforward manner. If she ever had a desire to marry again, then Pastor Whitaker would make a suitable candidate. However, she was not interested in going down that path ever again. She smoothed out her black mourning gown. "It has only been six months since Josh died. I require more time to mourn."

"Time has nothing to do with it, and you know it."

"It's true. Josh humiliated me with his antics."

The pastor took a step closer to her, his eyes filled with compassion. "You did nothing wrong. Josh deceived us all."

"Be that as it may be, I am not interested in being courted."

With a curt nod, Pastor Whitaker placed his black hat on his head. "You are in a ranching town full of men and few available women. It is in your best interest to select a man and marry him, at least for your own protection."

Her hand slipped into the pocket of her gown and gripped the derringer. She was not the type of woman who relied on a man to save her. "I thank you for your concern, but my brother sees to my protection." Pastor Whitaker opened his mouth, so she added, "Furthermore, our cowhands have been working for my family for years, and we trust them implicitly."

A frown came to his lips before he said, "I know we would suit, Darcy. Won't you at least consider my offer?"

Darcy took a step closer and softened her tone. "I have no doubt that we would get along fine, Jonathon. I know we've known each other since we were children, but I'm not ready." She reached out and touched the sleeve of his brown suit. "Frankly, I don't think I'll ever be ready."

He placed his hand on top of hers. "If you change your mind…" He let his words trail off as he allowed his hand to slide off hers and took a step back. "I will see you Sunday, won't I?"

"I will be there." She offered him a grateful smile.

He tipped his hat, turned, and walked down the porch steps towards the stable.

He was a good man, but Darcy never had any romantic feelings towards him. Growing up, she had always been in love with Josh Spencer. Her heart had never strayed from him. It had been the happiest day of her life when she married him, surrounded by her friends and loved ones. However, everything had changed the moment she said, "I do."

Her brother's voice came from the far end of the wrap-around porch. "Jonathon's right, you know."

She turned and responded dryly,

"Eavesdropping, Michael? I would have thought that was beneath you."

He chuckled. "You receive two marriage proposals a day, on average. It is hard not to overhear your conversations." He stepped closer to her, his spurs jingling. "Although, you were much nicer in your refusal of the good pastor."

Darcy watched as her would-be suitor rode down the dirt road and through the Shadow Ridge Ranch main gates. "He means well."

Crossing his arms over his blue work shirt, Michael leaned back against the railing. "You need to pick a suitor. There is a wide selection of men in town, and they are lining up to marry you. *Literally*," he teased.

"I have chosen a different path for my life," she stated firmly.

Michael wore a look of amusement. "Which is?"

Darcy took a deep breath to gather her courage before saying, "I have decided to become a Lady Pinkerton."

Her brother threw his head back and roared with laughter. Even when he'd calmed down, his eyes held mirth. "That was amusing, little sister."

"I'm serious," she replied, reaching into a pocket of her gown and pulling out a letter. "I have been corresponding with a Mr. Archie Gordon, who runs the Denver office, and I just received word that he is interested in hiring me."

"No!" Michael exclaimed, straightening from the railing. "You can't leave."

"I understand your reservations..."

He shouted over her. "My reservations? You want to move to Denver to become a Pinkerton agent! Of all your hare-brained ideas, this one is the worst."

Not deterred by her brother's anger, Darcy said, "My presence is not required here. You are perfectly capable of running Shadow Ridge Ranch on your own."

Michael turned and placed his hands on the railing, staring out towards the horizon. He didn't speak for a long moment. "You must be getting swindled, Darcy. That's the only explanation."

"I beg your pardon?"

"What qualifications do you have to be a Pinkerton agent?" he huffed.

"I'm a nurse," she reminded him. "I attended the prestigious Boston Female Medical College and completed my training. I also ran Josh's practice in town for a short while."

"Father sent you to that school only because you convinced

him that if you were a nurse, it would benefit the ranch," he argued.

"And it did."

Michael grunted. "This is foolhardy. I insist that you get this ridiculous notion out of your head."

"No," she stated, strengthening her resolve. "Mr. Gordon sent me a train ticket. I report in five days for the last round of interviews."

Her brother turned to face her. "You can't be serious."

"I am perfectly serious," she answered, placing the note back into her pocket.

"You intend to leave Shadow Ridge Ranch?" he asked in disbelief. "Leave me?"

Darcy reached up and touched the cameo on her lacy collar. "After I found out that Josh had been killed," she hesitated, pressing her lips together, "I saw an advertisement in the newspaper. The Pinkerton office in Denver wanted to hire female agents. So, I sat down and drafted a reply. A month later, I received a letter asking for additional information, and I followed up with a telegram."

"Did you tell this Mr. Gordon that you live on a ranch in the middle of New Mexico Territory?"

"I did. I was very honest about my background and my skills," she replied. "I didn't think that Mr. Gordon would even respond to my inquiry, but I am glad that he did."

Michael stared at her for a moment in stunned silence. "We need you on the ranch... I need you."

She shook her head, unconvinced. "You don't need me. Except for the occasional medical emergency, I spend my time riding across our lands or reading in my home. I'm bored."

"Why not travel? Go to Boston or New York?"

"I have been given a unique opportunity to discover what I am truly capable of. I want to go and see if I could be a Lady Pinkerton."

"You're already a nurse and part owner of a successful cattle ranch," her brother said. "You've already proven yourself."

"You're wrong. I need to strike out on my own."

Michael stepped closer and placed his hand on her right shoulder. "You were happy with your life before Josh died. Don't let him rob you of your future happiness, as well."

"It's true. I was content until I realized that nothing was what it seemed. I was duped, tricked, humiliated," she listed, "and living in this town, on this ranch, in my home, is too much. There are too many memories."

"You can come live with me and Anna at the big house," he attempted. "You don't have to remarry."

"No, I do not want to live with you and my sister-in-law," she said, turning her gaze back towards her small two-bedroom cottage. "If I stay here, the path is already laid out for me, and it's not the path I want to travel. I want to go to Denver and see if I can prove my worth as a Lady Pinkerton."

"I could have Sheriff Fisher arrest you," her stone-faced brother threatened.

She laughed at Michael's empty threat. "You wouldn't dare."

Her brother turned his gaze towards their expansive cattle ranch. "Mother and Father would be mortified if they were still alive. This is supposed to be our legacy."

"I didn't say I would never come back," she informed him. "I just need time away, and I think going to Denver is a good start."

He dropped his head and sighed. "Being a Pinkerton agent is dangerous. We've both read the newspapers and have heard the stories."

"I haven't even been officially hired yet. There is a chance I could arrive in Denver and botch the final interview," she informed him.

Michael smiled sadly. "We both know that you always get what you want."

"This has nothing to do with wanting to leave you."

"I know," he replied. "Just remember that this is your home, and you are always welcome back."

"Thank you."

A moment later, she found herself being swept into her brother's embrace. "I don't know what I would do if something happened to you, Darcy."

"I love you, too," she murmured against his chest. "Don't worry about me, I will find my way home… eventually."

Michael leaned back and smiled. "Perhaps your opinion of matrimony will change when you come back."

She returned his smile. "Never."

"Come," he said, placing his arm around her shoulder and tucking her up against him. "You get to be the one to tell Anna the horrible news." He shuddered. "She scares me when she gets riled up."

Darcy laughed, knowing her brother was not in earnest. Michael and Anna were deeply in love, and they had just announced that they were expecting a baby.

Her eyes strayed to the gated green fields with cattle lazily meandering about. The ripe, tangy odor of cow manure reached her nose. This was her home. Most everyone would call her crazy to leave this place. Here on Shadow Ridge Ranch, she had safety and security, but that wasn't enough, anymore. She needed to prove to herself that she could do more, be more.

Besides, she would rather become a Lady Pinkerton and deal with all kinds of low-lifes than marry again. At least with the criminals, you're allowed to shoot them.

Porter Shaw walked into the main house with a file in his hand. He had just solved a case where a young heiress had gone missing. It turned out that she had run away because her father had lowered her allowance. After informing the father that his daughter was at her friend's house, he had to sit down and begin the arduous process of writing up the report for Archie.

For the most part, he loved being a Pinkerton agent, but some of his cases were mundane, even boring. He preferred excitement and danger over repetitive and safe.

He veered towards the kitchen when the most delightful smell permeated the hall. As he walked into the kitchen, he saw Pearl, the housekeeper, wiping her hands off on her apron. "Would you like a cookie?" she asked as he approached the counter.

He gave her a boyish grin. "You know I can never refuse your cooking," he replied, taking the offered cookie.

"You are quite the charmer, Mr. Shaw," Pearl said, turning back towards the stove. She reached for a spoon and stirred the contents in the large pot.

Marianne hurried into the room and breathed a sigh of relief. "There you are, Porter. I've been looking everywhere for you." Strands of her red hair hung around her face, and her cheeks were pink from exertion.

He straightened to his full height, preparing to fight whatever problem that Marianne required. "Is everything all right?"

"Archie wants to see you right away," she announced, attempting to shoo him from the room. "He is quite insistent about it."

"Is that all?" he asked, reaching for another cookie.

Marianne grabbed his arm and started leading him towards Archie's office. "You must not keep him waiting any longer."

He towered over Archie's assistant, but he allowed her to escort him to his boss's office. All the agents had learned early on that Marianne was the glue that kept this office running smoothly. Furthermore, they were all placing bets on when Archie and Marianne would finally acknowledge their feelings for each other and get hitched.

Marianne knocked on the door before she opened it and pushed him in. "I found Porter."

"Finally!" the red-headed Irishman barked from behind his desk. His gaze softened as it landed on Marianne. "That will be all."

Marianne nodded and left the room as Porter stepped closer to the desk. A woman wearing a black dress, with a lacy collar and a cameo at the base of her throat, sat rigidly in a chair, facing Archie. She shifted her gaze towards him, and his feet faltered at her striking beauty. Her dark, brown hair was pulled back into a fancy chignon, but tendrils framed her face. She had a straight nose, a strong jaw, and lips that begged to be kissed. But her physical beauty was eclipsed by the fire in her eyes that spoke of an untold story. That mystery fascinated him.

Reluctantly turning his gaze back to Archie, Porter extended him the file. "Here is my report on the Rogers case."

Archie accepted the file and placed it on his desk. "Sit down, Mr. Shaw. We have much to discuss." Porter sat on the chair next to the woman. "I've just finished interviewing Mrs. Darcy Spencer, and I am partnering her with you on this next assignment."

Sneaking a glance at him, the woman asked, "May I ask why you picked Mr. Shaw to partner with me?"

"You may," Archie responded. "Mr. Porter Shaw is one of our top agents. He has successfully solved many of our most difficult cases in the Denver office."

Porter leaned forward in his seat. "Um… will I be required to marry her?" he asked, glancing over at Mrs. Spencer who pursed her lips in response.

Archie nodded. "Yes, the same rules apply. You will marry

Mrs. Spencer and train her on her first assignment. After the training is complete, you may seek an annulment, or continue working as a partnership."

Porter shifted in his seat to face the lovely Mrs. Darcy Spencer. "And you agreed to this... willingly?"

"I'm still here, aren't I?" she replied with a forced smile.

Attempting to disarm her, Porter offered his most charming smile, one that worked on all the ladies. "I have no doubt that we will get along nicely."

Mrs. Spencer visibly stiffened. "I am not looking to see if we suit, Mr. Shaw. I'm here only because I want to be trained as an agent."

Archie chuckled. "Besides being impervious to your charms, Mrs. Spencer is a trained nurse and is a part owner of a cattle ranch. Which is why I assigned her to this case." He reached for a file on his desk and opened it up. "Mr. Adam McCoy, owner of McCoy Cattle Ranch, has hired us because his cowhands are disappearing."

"Disappearing?" Porter questioned.

"Yes. In the past six weeks, four men have gone missing, and Mr. McCoy suspects foul play," Archie confirmed.

Porter opened his mouth to ask his next question, but Mrs. Spencer spoke up first. "Why does he suspect foul play?"

"As you are aware, securing the fences are vital for these

cattle ranches, and his ranch hands scour the fences daily to look for any signs of weaknesses. However, some of these men fail to report back," Archie explained. "Their horses and equipment are found intact, there is no sign of a struggle, but the men are nowhere to be found."

Mrs. Spencer nodded. "That does seem odd. There was a time when one of our ranch hands was killed by a mountain lion, but there was an obvious sign of a struggle."

"Does Mr. McCoy suspect any of his competitors?" Porter asked.

"Everyone is a suspect at this point," Archie said, extending him the file. "McCoy Cattle Ranch is near a small, bustling town called Aurora's Creek, CO. The ranch is approximately sixty miles north of Denver. A wagon is waiting out front and will take you to the train station. Once you arrive at Aurora's Creek, you will have to secure a wagon and travel to the ranch. You should arrive in about six hours, barring any unforeseen circumstances."

Porter accepted the file and opened it. "When does Mr. McCoy expect us?"

Archie pulled out his pocket watch and replied, "Before dusk."

"We will have to leave immediately," Porter murmured.

"That would be wise," Archie agreed, returning his pocket

watch to his vest's pocket. "For this assignment, Mrs. Spencer will be hired on as the housekeeper," he paused, turning his gaze towards him, "and you will be a ranch hand. This will allow Mr. McCoy to easily explain your sudden presence."

"Understood," Porter stated, rising. He extended his hand towards Mrs. Spencer. "Shall we?"

"Aren't you forgetting something, agent?" Archie asked in wry amusement.

Porter froze as realization dawned. He knew this moment was coming, but now it seemed unreal. Could he marry a woman that he had only met moments ago? True, this marriage would be in name only, but he had been taught that a marriage was a life-long commitment.

Mrs. Spencer must have felt his hesitation because she slipped her gloved hand into his and he felt a surge of protectiveness wash over him. His trademark impish smile came to his lips as he helped her to rise. "Are you ready to get married, darling?"

She yanked her hand back. "I am not your *darling*, Mr. Shaw."

"Does that mean I won't get to kiss my bride?" he teased, stepping closer.

"You presume correctly," she declared, tilting her face up defiantly.

Looking down at her flawless skin, Porter had a sudden urge to run his thumb across her high cheekbones. "Pity. At least for you," he teased. "I have been told that I am a remarkable kisser."

Mrs. Spencer arched an eyebrow. "I highly doubt that."

He leaned closer and whispered next to her ear, "I bet by the end of this assignment, you will be begging to kiss me."

"I think not," she stated icily.

He shrugged as he leaned back. "I think so."

Mrs. Spencer's hand lowered and slid into the pocket of her gown, but it stopped when Archie said, "Are you ready to get hitched?"

Chapter 2

As they bounced along in the wagon down the rough road, Darcy ran her hand down the length of the new traveling gown that Marianne had provided for her. It was lavender with a white lacy collar and full skirt, trimmed with ruching along the back. It felt odd to be out of her mourning clothes, but she couldn't very well continue the practice. Not only was she newly married, but she was a Pinkerton agent. A mourning newlywed would raise suspicion.

She snuck a glance at her new temporary husband. He was well over six feet tall, with intense blue eyes, chiseled features, and brown hair. His muscular physique was only enhanced by his engaging personality, which exuded confidence and a touch of cockiness.

They hadn't spoken more than a few words to each other since leaving Archie's office. The train had offered them no privacy, and she found herself in no rush to speak to Porter. He made her feel uneasy.

Porter's voice broke through her musings. "That color suits you."

"Thank you," she said, her hand moving to hold on to the side of the wagon.

He glanced her way. "You must have loved your husband very much to honor him by wearing mourning attire."

"I did, very much," she hesitated, "once."

Shifting his gaze back to the road, Porter appeared deep in thought. Finally, he spoke again. "I know this is an awkward situation for both of us, being married and all…"

"We are only married until you train me, and we complete this assignment. After that, we go our separate ways."

"Good. We are in agreement then."

"Good," she replied.

Porter surprised her by shifting the reins to his left hand and draping his right arm over the bench. "It would be best if I start your lessons." His eyes darted occasionally towards the road, but he kept his focus on her. "Always keep your gun near you. Trust no one and assume everyone is lying to you."

Darcy bristled at his blunt words. She knew that truth all too well. "That will not be an issue."

"Archie assigned Bailey as our surname, and we will retain our given names." He was silent for a moment, then asked,

"Why did you want to become a Pinkerton agent?"

Darcy debated about lying to him, but that would not be a logical response. They were supposed to trust each other as partners, and a lie would not benefit her. "After Josh, my husband... er... my previous husband, died, I ran across the advertisement in the newspaper. The words appeared to fly off the page, and it seemed like a sign. Destiny." Her eyes scanned over the rocky terrain. "I know that must sound ludicrous to someone like you."

"Not at all. After my family's cattle ranch was foreclosed on, I drifted from place to place until I ended up in Chicago. I had read an article about how Pinkerton agents had thwarted a bank robbery, and I decided in that moment that I wanted to be an agent."

"I am sorry about your family's cattle ranch," she murmured. "I couldn't imagine losing my family's legacy."

A wistful look came over Porter's expression. "I had a wonderful childhood at that ranch, but we had ongoing feuds with our neighbors about watering and grazing rights. Eventually, it became too much, but my father refused to sell to any of those '*backstabbers*', as he called them," he huffed. "His gnawing hate drove us kids away, and he died a short time later... alone."

"How long ago was that?"

"Eight years."

Keeping her gaze on his, she asked, "Do you mind if I ask how old you are?"

"Not at all. I am twenty-eight."

"Oh," she replied. "I'm twenty-five."

He smirked. "I wondered about that, but I am smart enough not to ask a woman her age."

"Wise man," she joked.

"Tell me about your cattle ranch," he said, his alert eyes scanning the trees along the road.

"Like you, I have fond memories of my childhood at Shadow Ridge Ranch," she shared. "It's one of the largest cattle ranches in the New Mexico Territory, and the land has been in my family for generations. My mother died when I was young, and my father had no idea how to raise a daughter. So, I was treated like my brother until my fifteenth birthday. I even wore trousers and went on cattle drives."

"What happened when you were fifteen?"

Darcy laughed lightly. "My grandmother came to visit and was aghast when she saw me rounding up the cattle with the cowhands. She demanded that I start wearing dresses and be sent off to a proper finishing school."

"And were you?"

She shifted towards him. "I was. That is where I discovered

my love for books and learning."

"Is that why you wanted to become a nurse?" he asked.

"In a way," Darcy replied vaguely. There were still some things she was not willing to share. She glanced sideways at her new husband and was disconcerted to see him watching her. It seemed as though he knew she was keeping something from him.

"So, you are a lady, a nurse, and a part-time ranch hand. Did I miss anything?" he asked after a moment, a smile on his lips.

"That rounds it up nicely," she said, returning his smile, grateful he hadn't pressed her for her secrets.

His face grew expressionless as he inquired, "Did your husband die during the war?"

She bit her tongue, holding back her retort. "No. He was killed during a shoot-out."

"Was he a lawman?"

"No. A doctor," she replied, her words curt.

"When did he pass?"

She pressed her lips tightly together before answering, "Six months ago."

"How long were you married?" he asked, his gaze focusing on the road.

"A little more than two years." Her answer may have been

vague, but she knew exactly how long she had been married to Josh. It had been two years, two months, and ten days.

Darcy shifted in her seat, turning slightly away from Porter. She hoped to be done with these questions about her former husband. She did not enjoy speaking of Josh's betrayal. They were supposed to have children and live happily ever after.

Porter must have misconstrued her reluctance to talk as a sign of affection because a sad smile crossed his face. "I understand. It must be too painful to speak of him."

"The memories are too raw," she admitted. At least that was the truth.

Porter nodded. "Well, we have two more hours till we arrive at the McCoy's ranch. What would you like to talk about?"

Her eyes shifted towards the reins. "May I drive the team?"

A playful gleam came to Porter's eyes. "But you are a woman."

"I am glad that you noticed," she replied, surprising herself with that flirtatious comment.

His eyes roamed her face, and one corner of his mouth curled into an approving smile. "Oh, I noticed, Mrs. Shaw."

Darcy felt her cheeks growing increasingly warm, and she turned her attention back towards the road. Porter scooted closer and extended her the reins. "I am just teasing you. I am more than happy to relinquish control over to you."

"Thank you." She accepted the reins and his fingers brushed up against hers, causing a momentary tingle that she was quick to ignore.

Feeling the need to distance herself from Porter, she pressed up against the side of the bench. He gave her an understanding look and slid over to create more distance between them. How could a man that she had just met be able to read her emotions so well?

Well, he was a Pinkerton agent, she rationalized. That must come naturally.

Porter was no fool. It was clear that his wife was hiding something about her dead husband. But what could it be? Whenever Josh was mentioned, Darcy's answers became short and aggressive.

His right arm draped casually over the bench, and he was angled towards his wife. *His wife.* Beauty-wise she was perfect. He could never tire of her beautiful features and bewitching eyes. But marriage was based on more than physical attraction. More importantly, this marriage was not real. It was in name only.

A smile graced Darcy's lips as she urged the horses faster up a long hill. "Are you enjoying yourself?" he asked.

"I am." She glanced over at him. "How are you enjoying your leisurely ride?"

He grinned. "I daresay that you are the first woman that has ever offered to drive a wagon for me."

"How many siblings do you have?"

His eyes focused on the towering trees, looking for any signs of danger. "I have two brothers."

"Where are they now?" she asked, shifting the reins in her hands.

"My brothers work at a cattle ranch somewhere in the Wyoming Territory. I haven't seen them in almost eight years."

She turned her gaze towards him, and her eyes held compassion. "Don't you miss them?"

"Every day." Porter noticed that Darcy's once white gloves were now darkened with dirt and grime. He pointed at the reins. "Would you like me to take over, so you don't ruin your gloves?"

She shook her head. "Gloves can be washed, Mr. Shaw."

"Porter," he corrected.

"I suppose I will need to say your given name in public," she murmured.

He reached out and touched her sleeve, causing her to jerk backwards. "Darcy," he stated in a chiding tone. "We need to appear affectionate towards one another."

"Not all marriages have love between them," she muttered under her breath.

Surprised by her response, he questioned, "Did your marriage lack love?"

She stiffened. "That is rather a personal question."

He took his finger and played with the lace along the edges of her sleeves. "Not if we are married."

"But we are not truly married."

"We are, and I have the document to prove it." He brought his hand up to pat his vest pocket. Why did he feel the need to tease this high-strung woman?

Porter watched as Darcy's hand began slipping towards a pocket in her gown. "May I ask what you carry in your right front pocket?" he asked.

Darcy looked over at him with wide eyes. "Why do you suppose I have something in my pocket?"

"Because I've noticed your hand gravitates towards that pocket whenever I tease you," he revealed.

"Oh, I suppose I do," she mumbled. "It's a habit that I picked up after I got married."

"Which was?"

Darcy pulled a derringer from her pocket. "I always carry a

gun for protection."

Porter straightened, suddenly angry. "You started carrying a gun *after* you were married?"

She returned the pistol to her pocket. "My husband was not what he seemed."

"Was he a criminal?" he found himself asking.

The same vacant stare came into her eyes, and he could see her erecting walls around her. "No. He was a law-abiding citizen."

"Did he hurt you?"

She turned away from him, but not before he caught the sadness that marred her face. "It depends on how you define 'hurt'."

"Darcy… I…" he started, unsure of how to comfort her.

Pulling back on the reins, Darcy stopped the team of horses in the middle of the road. "Excuse me. I need a moment alone," she murmured, extending him the reins. She didn't say another word as she hopped off the carriage.

Porter watched her walk swiftly towards the cover of the trees. It was evident that Josh had not been a devoted husband, and it would take more than one conversation for Darcy to open up. As much as he wanted her to confide in him, they didn't have time to lollygag. They needed to arrive at the cattle ranch and discover why men were disappearing. That was his job.

That was *their* job. Learning Darcy's secret was secondary to the case.

He was a Pinkerton agent, first, and foremost.

An Agent for Darcy

Chapter 3

Darcy smelled and heard the cows before she saw them in the distance. She breathed in the familiar scent.

Porter huffed in amusement. "Did you just smile when you took in a deep breath?"

"I have always associated this smell with happiness," she admitted, not even remotely embarrassed by her reaction.

He gave her a look of disbelief. "You associate manure with happiness?"

"Don't you?" she challenged.

"Fair enough," he conceded. "It does remind me of a happier time, as well."

Her eyes roamed the ranch as she continued to drive the wagon down the dirt road. Fenced pastures lined both sides of the road leading up to a large, white house with a wrap-around porch and a red barn off to the side. As they approached the house, Darcy saw wilted flowers in the flowerbed.

Darcy pulled the wagon to a stop in front of the home. Once she set the brake, Porter hopped down and walked over to her side. "Remember to be cautious of your surroundings at all times." He gave her a private smile. "It is time to play the role of a happily married couple."

She placed her hands on his shoulders and allowed him to assist her down. "Don't worry about me. I have learned to play that role quite well."

The door to the house opened with a creak. An attractive man, not much older than she, walked out to the porch, drying his hands with a white cloth. His shirt and dark trousers fit tightly against his body, highlighting his muscular frame. His blonde hair and square jaw accented his commanding presence.

"Can I help you?" he asked.

Porter stood next to her. "We are looking for Mr. McCoy."

The man tossed the cloth onto his right shoulder. "You found him, but I prefer to be called Adam." With a charming smile, he directed his next question towards her. "And who might you be?"

Darcy found herself smiling back at Mr. McCoy. "My name is…"

She heard a low growl before Porter cut her off. "We are Mr. and Mrs. Bailey." He placed his right hand on the small of her back and ushered her closer to the porch. "We are your new housekeeper and cowhand."

"Ah, I should have known." Adam's eyes flashed with disappointment. "Please come inside."

Porter escorted her into the home and asked in a hushed voice, "Did you forget the part where we are happily married?"

"I remember," she assured him as her eyes roamed the house. It wasn't overly dirty, but a fine coat of dust covered all the furniture.

She could feel Porter's warm breath on her ear. "Then will you refrain from flirting with our client."

Darcy stopped in the hall and glared up at him. "I did no such thing. How dare you accuse me of that!" She felt a need to defend herself but kept her voice low.

"I know what I saw," he insisted.

Her eyes narrowed at her infuriating partner, but she did not feel the need to dignify his words with a response. She huffed and started walking towards the back of the home. However, before she could take her second step, Porter's hand grabbed her arm from behind. "You must remember that you are a Pinkerton agent, first and foremost."

"Thank you for that sound advice," she replied dryly. "Will you kindly release my arm?"

When Porter removed his hand, Darcy squared her shoulders and walked into the kitchen. Her steps faltered at the sight in front of her. Plates, dishes, and utensils covered the length of the counterspace. More dirty dishes were stacked on the ground near the sink and next to the door sat an enormous pile of laundry.

Adam was leaning up against the wall near the table and offered her an apologetic smile. "I am not sure which I need more... a housekeeper or a Pinkerton agent."

"Good thing you have both," Porter said as he brushed past her into the room, completely oblivious to her outrage.

Darcy's jaw dropped. She hadn't been hired on to be a Pinkerton agent. She had been hired to clean while Porter handled the investigation. Of all the cruel tricks that had befallen her, this was the one that hurt the most. The agency had deceived her. What was worse, her brother had been right. She'd been duped.

In a relatively calm voice, she spoke up. "I apologize Mr. McCoy, but I am afraid there has been a big misunderstanding. I have decided not to accept this case."

Porter pivoted towards her with a look of confusion. "Can you repeat that, *wife*?"

"I will drive into town and acquire a hotel room for the night," Darcy explained. "After that, I will see myself back to Denver and stay until you complete the assignment." She tilted her head towards Adam. "I apologize for the inconvenience, Mr. McCoy."

Without saying a word, Porter grabbed her arm and led her towards a room off the kitchen. Once inside, he let go, turned to face her, and demanded, "Do you want to explain what you think you are doing?"

"I thought it was fairly obvious," she responded. "I am quitting."

"Why? We just got here," he said through gritted teeth.

She clasped her hands in front of her, not even remotely deterred by Porter's anger directed at her. "The agency didn't hire me to be an agent."

Porter gave her a baffled look. "Of course they did! My job is to train you."

She stepped closer to him, and she was now toe-to-toe with him. "No. I was hired to clean and cook. Not to be an agent. I was duped, *again*."

Now, Porter's jaw dropped. "Is that what the issue is? There are too many dishes for you to clean?" he asked in a sarcastic tone. "I knew hiring women was a mistake."

Pointing towards the kitchen, she explained, "It will take me at least two days to clean all those dishes, and another day to do the laundry. How am I supposed to work as an agent if my hands are literally covered with soapy water?"

Porter placed his hands on her shoulders. "Have you considered that you are inside the house to protect Mr. McCoy?

He might be a target, as well."

"Do not attempt to pacify me, Mr. Shaw," she asserted, shaking off his hands. "I feel foolish enough as it is."

His brows furrowed. "Why would you feel foolish?"

"I spoke to you of destiny, but obviously, I was only hired to be a servant." As hard as she tried, she couldn't prevent her voice from hitching with emotion.

Immediately, Porter wrapped his arms around her and pulled her close. "You were hired because of your knowledge of a working cattle ranch. It could prove vital to our investigation."

"How does cleaning help our case?"

"Being an agent requires us to go undercover from time to time," he pointed out. "While you are posing as a housekeeper, I will be outside with the other cowhands doing back-breaking work."

She tilted her head up to look at him. "Can we switch roles? I would much rather work as a cowhand than clean all those dishes."

"Why am I not surprised by that question?" Porter grinned, tightening his hold on her.

Darcy closed her eyes as she rested her head against his chest. It felt so natural to be in his arms, to be comforted. Perhaps she was being foolhardy in her assessment. Suddenly, her heart dropped, and she stiffened in his arms. She was the same foolish woman, lowering her inhibitions because a man charmed her. Taking a step back, she said, "I still…"

Porter cut her off as he started to roll up the sleeves of his white shirt. "To prove to you that you have come to the wrong conclusion about only being hired to keep house, I will help you clean the kitchen."

"You?"

He gave her an impish grin. "I do know how to clean, Mrs. Shaw."

"You would do that?" she asked, her eyes searching his. "For me?"

He shoved the sleeves above his elbows before asking, "If I help you clean the kitchen, will you stay on as my partner?" His eyes held vulnerability.

Touched beyond words by his kind gesture, she found herself nodding. "I will."

"Well, wife… let's get to work."

The sun was setting when Mr. McCoy walked back into the kitchen holding two bowls. "I figured you both could use some supper," he paused with a knowing look, "and a break." He looked down at the contents in the bowls. "It looks inedible, but the cook does make a good chili."

Porter straightened up and placed his hand on his back. After stretching for a few moments, he accepted the bowls from Adam. "Thank you," he said. "Darcy, come and eat."

Darcy lifted her head up from the pan she had been scrubbing. She wiped her forearm across her forehead. "Why do you have so many blasted dishes, Mr. McCoy?"

Surprised by Darcy's abrupt question, Porter couldn't control the laugh that escaped his lips.

"I do apologize, and please call me Adam," Mr. McCoy said as he sat down. "My wife died two weeks ago, and I haven't touched the dishes since then."

Darcy's hand stilled on the pan as her eyes grew compassionate. "I am sorry for your loss." She placed the pan into the hot water. "What did she die from?"

"We don't rightly know," Adam replied. "Two weeks ago, I took a group of the cowhands to the eastern tip of my property to search for missing cattle, and it took longer than intended. I returned home the following morning, and found Amanda lying dead on the floor in the kitchen, surrounded by," he hesitated, looking uncomfortable, "bodily fluids."

"Like diarrhea and vomiting?" Darcy asked without a hint of embarrassment.

Adam frowned as he added, "And blood. Lots of blood."

"What did the doctor rule as her cause of death?" Darcy pressed.

Adam dropped his right forearm onto the table. "He said she died of cholera."

"Cholera?" Porter repeated in surprise.

Adam nodded. "A large group of Russian emigrants came to Aurora's Creek to settle temporarily in unoccupied buildings throughout the town. Dr. Wilcox has been overwhelmed by the number of deaths among the emigrants. It has been widely assumed that they brought the cholera with them."

Darcy bit her lower lip. "How did your wife have contact with these Russian emigrants?"

"Amanda had gone into town a few days prior to buy some items at the mercantile. Perhaps she had contact with them then," Adam suggested.

Darcy looked closely at all the plates that contained scraps of food and tea cups. "Did you notice whether Amanda's breath smelled like garlic or bitter almonds?"

"No," Adam replied. "Why?"

Picking up a glass, Darcy held it up to the candle, squinting her eyes as she analyzed the contents. "Had she complained of abdominal cramps before you left?" she asked, returning the glass to the counter.

Adam sat straight up in his seat with a perplexed expression on his face. "Not that I recall."

"You don't think…" Porter asked, putting his spoon down.

"It would make sense." Darcy picked up a teacup that lay near the back of the counter and reached for a spoon. She stirred the tea for a moment, her eyes fixated on the liquid. "Was this your wife's tea?"

"It was. That was her grandmother's teacup," Adam confirmed. "Amanda abhorred coffee."

A deep frown came to Darcy's lips. "I'm sorry to tell you this, Adam, but your wife was murdered."

"No! I don't believe it!" Adam shouted. "Who would want to kill my wife?"

Holding the teacup in her hand, Darcy walked over and placed it on the table next to Porter. "White arsenic powder has no taste and is odorless," she hesitated, "but, it isn't soluble. It must be dissolved in tea or something hot. When the liquid starts to cool, some will precipitate out, and you might see or even taste strange particles."

She took the spoon and placed it into the tea. Lifting the spoon, there were floating particles in the liquid. "In our medical books, it says that if these gritty particles are eaten, they will taste like sand."

Adam cast her a questioning look. "How do you know so

much about arsenic?"

"My wife is a nurse," Porter announced proudly.

"A nurse?" Adam repeated in confusion. "Then, why are you a Pinkerton agent?"

"That is a story for another day," Darcy replied. "Stomach cramps, diarrhea, and vomiting are all classic signs of arsenic poisoning. If you would allow me to exhume the body, then I could confirm my diagnosis."

"Absolutely not!" Adam exclaimed.

Porter pushed aside his bowl, suddenly losing his appetite. "Who benefits from your wife's death?"

Adam looked stunned. "No one," he stated firmly.

"Think," Porter urged. "Why would someone want to kill your wife and four of your cowhands?"

"I don't know!" Adam jumped up from his seat. "How do we even know Amanda's death is connected to the cowhands' disappearances?"

"They are related, because I don't believe in coincidences," Porter declared.

"Who gets the ranch if you die?" Darcy pressed.

"My brother, Ralph," Adam revealed, "but he loved Amanda. He wouldn't have harmed her. Why would he?"

"Was Ralph with you when you went to search for the

missing cattle?" Darcy asked.

Adam shook his head. "No, he stayed behind," he put his hands up in front of him, "but that's not unusual. He was branding the calves that weekend."

"Did you tell anyone that you hired Pinkerton agents to investigate the missing cowhands?" Porter asked.

"Per Mr. Gordon's instructions, I only informed my staff that I hired a new cowhand and a housekeeper," Adam stated, running his fingers through his hair.

"That's good," Porter said. "From now on, you do not eat or drink anything that someone offers you, even if they take a bite or sip first. People have been known to build up an immunity to arsenic powder."

Darcy came to stand next to him, gently placing her hand on his shoulder, but her comments were directed towards Adam. "If you exhibit any signs of arsenic poisoning, then please, seek me out immediately."

Adam turned away from them and clasped his hands around the back of his head. "I can't believe this. Someone murdered my wife. I suspected something happened to my ranch hands, but Amanda…" He broke off as a large sob overtook him. After a moment, he turned back to face them. "Who would do such a thing?"

"That is what we are going to find out," Porter assured him.

"We won't rest until we discover who is behind this and why."

Darcy stepped over to Adam and asked, "May I see your hands?" He extended them with his palms down. She examined his fingernails. "Good. You don't appear to be suffering from long term exposure to arsenic."

Adam stepped back, the anguish clearly on his features. "Excuse me… I… uh… need some time alone," he stammered, turning and walking away from them. Reaching the door, he spun back around. "You are staying in the foreman's cottage just down the road. It is painted brown. You can't miss it."

"We don't mean to intrude on your foreman's home," Darcy said.

Adam frowned. "He was one of the first men who went missing. I don't think he will mind."

After Adam left, Darcy sat down next to Porter. "We will need to preserve this evidence for when we involve the sheriff."

Porter looked at the teacup, noting the floating particles. "Are you sure?" he asked in a hesitant tone.

"I am," Darcy confirmed. "White arsenic powder has been an effective way to kill for centuries. In medical school, we were trained to look for the signs of arsenic poisoning, because it's so easily mistaken for food poisoning, dysentery, or cholera. The earlier you catch it, the greater the chance of survival."

"Do you believe him?" Porter's eyes focused on the door

that Adam just walked through.

Darcy looked puzzled. "You don't?"

"I didn't say that," Porter replied, "but you must always stay objective. Adam could have easily killed his wife and tried to pass it off as a natural death."

"He seemed genuinely heartbroken. I can't imagine he had anything to do with his wife's murder."

"I agree." Porter gave a decisive head bob. "However, as a Pinkerton agent, you will discover that people will kill for the most asinine reasons. There are the usual motives: greed, betrayal, and secrets, not to mention crimes of passion and circumstance."

Darcy looked at him with tender green eyes, and he detected a glimpse of pity. "Does that not weigh heavily on your conscience, investigating all those crimes?"

"I have learned to distance myself from the victims," Porter explained.

"That sounds lonely."

Porter rose from his chair and placed his bowl in the sink. "It's practical. You must learn how to separate your personal life from your life as an agent. If they ever merge, it would be too much for even the most seasoned agent to cope with." After cleaning the bowl, he turned around and leaned back against the counter. "We should head down to the cottage and get some rest. It will be a long day tomorrow for both of us."

"I think that's wise," she agreed.

"Are you hungry?"

Darcy looked longingly at the bowl of chili still on the table. "I am, but I don't dare eat it."

That didn't surprise him. "Stay there. I will find something to cook for you." She started to rise, but stopped when he insisted, "Allow me to take care of you, Mrs. Shaw."

Her eyes went wide, and she looked at him with what could only be described as adoration. "You wish to cook *me* dinner?"

"It's only dinner," he responded.

However, by the look on her face, it was clear that she didn't consider this a small task. "Thank you," she murmured as she leaned back in her chair.

Porter couldn't be sure, but he swore he saw her blink back tears.

An Agent for Darcy

Chapter 4

Darcy smelled the pancakes before her eyes even opened. What a delightful way to wake up, she thought. The sun had barely peeked over the horizon when she threw back her covers and stepped out of the bed. She removed her nightgown and dressed herself in a simple calico gown with no lace or frills, which was designed for the rigors of the Wild West.

She quickly brushed her hair, pulling it back into a bun at the base of her neck, and put her boots on. It was time to face Porter. After he had prepared her eggs for supper, Darcy had felt something shift between them. They were not quite friends yet, but they weren't adversaries anymore.

Exiting her room, she walked the short distance to the kitchen. The small cottage had a kitchen, sitting area and bedroom. The sound of sizzling butter in the pan greeted her as she rounded the corner and saw Porter flipping a pancake in the air. "Did they teach you that at the agency?" she joked.

He glanced over his shoulder at her with a twinkle in his

eye. "Finally, sleeping beauty has awoken for the day."

"It is barely sunrise," she contested, looking out the small square window in the kitchen.

Dropping a pancake onto a plate, Porter replied, "I've been up for over an hour."

Darcy took a moment to admire Porter's brown trousers, long-sleeved plaid shirt, black vest and a red bandana handkerchief tied around his neck in a hard knot. She had to admit that he looked ruggedly handsome in his cowboy attire.

Porter whistled, causing her eyes to dart up to meet his gloating gaze. "Do you like what you see, Mrs. Shaw?"

"I… um…" Her words faded as she cleared her throat in utter embarrassment.

He was standing next to the round table with a plate in his hand. "I have asked you, twice, now, if you are ready for your breakfast," he stated with an impish grin. "But you couldn't seem to stop ogling me."

"I wasn't ogling you," she defended.

"You are a terrible liar," he teased before placing the plate on the table. "I suppose it will be incredibly difficult for you to get work done since you have been partnered with such an attractive man."

"Am I being reassigned then?" she asked innocently.

"Touché." He laughed as he pulled out a chair for her. "Come sit down and eat before it gets cold."

She sat down and allowed him to push in her chair. "Supper and now breakfast. You are spoiling me."

"That is the idea." Porter went back over to the stove and started preparing more pancakes. "Didn't your husband ever make you food?"

Darcy reached for her fork as she revealed, "No. Josh wasn't the kind to spoil anyone."

"Even his wife?" he asked with an uplifted brow.

"No." She poured syrup on her pancakes and started eating, ignoring Porter's watchful eye.

"Darcy, I am your partner, and I need to know more about you. Please stop avoiding my questions," he requested, shifting towards her as he cooked.

"Ask me anything, except about Josh. I do not like to discuss my husband."

"Dead husband," he corrected, pointing the spatula at her, "and you need to."

She swallowed her bite. "Why is that?"

He removed the pancakes from the pan, placed them onto an empty plate, and walked them over to the table. "Because I need to know everything about you to be an effective partner.

Your likes and dislikes, fears and joys, and anything from your past that might affect your work." He pulled out a chair and sat down. "Both of us need to know each other so well that we can begin anticipating each other's next move."

After taking a bite of food, Darcy chewed slowly as she chose her next words carefully. "Josh is a touchy subject for me."

"I understand, but this is not a suggestion," he said. "Let's start with an easy question. How did you two meet?"

Placing her fork on the plate, she sighed then shared, "From the moment I saw Josh in the school house, I knew he was the one. He was three years older than me, and I used to follow him around everywhere he went." She smiled sadly. "I even told him that he was going to marry me one day."

"What happened?" he asked before he took a large bite of his pancakes.

Her eyes darted towards the plain white walls. "I went off to finishing school and Josh continued his education to become a doctor, eventually ending up at Boston University. When I arrived back in town after completing school, I convinced my father to send me to a medical school in Boston, just so I could be closer to him."

Porter swallowed his bite. "I take it that worked."

"Not at first," she confessed. "I was so busy with my studies that we rarely saw each other during my first six months, but we shared the same group of friends from doing rounds at the nearby hospital. Josh was in his final year of school and spent a considerable amount of time enjoying the nightlife. There were many days that he was too drunk to go to his classes, and his roommates were forced to take notes."

"I can see why you fancied the man," Porter joked.

"I deserve that." Darcy picked up her fork and pushed the pancake around on her plate. "I should have seen the signs, but I thought I could save him from himself. Help him become a better man." Her fork stilled. "He was brilliant when he was sober."

"You sacrificed yourself to save him," Porter stated, pointing his fork at her.

She winced at the truthfulness of his words. "When we arrived back in town, I decided to give him time to set up his practice, and I spent most of my time at my family's cattle ranch," she shared, placing her fork back on her plate. "But Josh was a charmer and after a while he began pursuing me. He bought me flowers, chocolate, and made me promises that he never intended to keep."

Darcy rose and placed the plate on the counter before she found the strength to continue. "After we were married, Josh became a different person. He started controlling me, forcing me to do certain things, and if I refused, he would become exceedingly angry."

Porter's jaw clenched. "Did he ever strike you?"

"Only once," she confessed, returning to her seat. For some reason, being close to Porter provided her with much needed reassurance. "After he knocked me to the ground, I told him that I would shoot him if he ever laid a hand on me again."

"That's why you carry the derringer."

"Eventually, it didn't matter. Josh would go to the saloon and drink excessively every night." She ducked her head, embarrassed. "I started sleeping in another room and would lock the door to avoid his drunken temper."

Porter placed his hand on her sleeve. "Why didn't you tell your father or brother?"

"I couldn't," she stated with a shake of her head. "I kept thinking it would get better, especially since we got along fine when Josh wasn't drunk."

"A marriage shouldn't be about merely getting along fine."

"Most mornings, I would handle the patients until Josh arrived, and no one seemed the wiser."

His warm hand encompassed hers as he asked, "How did he die?"

Darcy felt the blood drain from her face. She couldn't answer that. She wouldn't answer that. Luckily, she was saved by a knock at the door. "I'll get it," she said, jumping up from her seat.

"Wait," Porter declared. "Where is your gun?"

Her eyes darted towards the back room. "In my nightstand."

He frowned, obviously displeased with her response. "A Pinkerton agent always carries a weapon. *Always.*"

"I understand." She hesitated. "Should I retrieve it now?"

"Wait till after our guest leaves." He stood and walked towards the door. "While you were sleeping the morning away..."

"I was hardly sleeping the morning... " she attempted to say.

Porter spoke over her in an amused tone. "I invited our boss for breakfast." He smirked, and her gaze dropped to his lips.

What was wrong with her, she wondered, as she quickly averted her gaze. She was acting like a love-sick debutante instead of the jaded widow that she was.

Tearing his eyes away from his beautiful wife, Porter opened the door wide. "Good morning, sir." His greeting dimmed when he noticed the dark circles under Mr. McCoy's eyes. "Come in," he urged as his eyes scanned the empty yard.

"Morning," Adam mumbled under his breath as he brushed past him.

Darcy spoke up from her seat. "It appears that you had a rough evening."

Adam grunted as he dropped into a chair. "I just discovered that my wife was murdered. How do you think I slept last night?"

Rather than appear upset by his angry tone, Darcy gave him a sympathetic smile. "Allow me to serve you breakfast." She rose, grabbed a plate from the counter, and dumped a pile of pancakes from the plate on the table onto it. "Here you go," she said cheerfully, offering him the pancakes.

Adam winced as he accepted the plate. "I am sorry for being so rude."

"You have nothing to apologize for," she assured him before she sat back down.

Porter noticed that Darcy wore a simple dress for the day, but it only enhanced her natural beauty. How was it possible that she looked radiant from the moment she woke up? When she'd stepped into the kitchen this morning, the whole room brightened.

Banishing his wayward thoughts, he sat in a chair across from Adam. "Before I report for work, would you explain to us what is going on at your ranch?"

Picking up his fork, Adam started, "I own thousands of acres, and my property backs up into the foothills of the Rocky Mountains. Obviously, my entire property is not fenced, but along the north-west corner of my property there is a lush valley surrounded by towering mountains. My father constructed a fence along one area to prevent the cattle from disappearing up one of the mountain trails."

Adam stopped speaking and took a large bite of his pancakes. After he swallowed his food, he continued. "I own over one thousand head of cattle, and we routinely rotate the cattle for grazing purposes. My foreman is constantly sending cowhands to check the fences and make any necessary repairs. About six weeks ago, Trevor was responsible for checking on the fences in the valley and never came home."

"Did you search for him?"

Adam nodded. "The following morning, we mounted a search, but we couldn't find him or find any type of a struggle. His horse and gear had been secured to a post, making the situation even more peculiar. How can someone just disappear?"

Porter leaned forward in his seat. "He might have fallen off a cliff or got swept away in a flash flood."

"We considered those possibilities," Adam stated. "However, the following week, Nick, my foreman, went missing under the same circumstances."

"Did you consider sending the cowhands in pairs?" Darcy asked.

Pushing his plate away, Adam said, "Yes, and they disappeared as well. The next day, I sent a telegram asking the Pinkerton Detective Agency to take my case."

"Have you considered the Indians might have ambushed these men?" Porter questioned.

"Anything is possible. Lately, a few tribes have been feuding over land," Adam expressed, "but they have been hunting game on my family's property for generations. My men are under strict orders not to engage the Indians and to let them pass in peace. Besides, they are more interested in the elk, buffalo, and bighorn sheep anyway."

Porter rested his right forearm onto the table. "What about a competitor?"

Adam shook his head. "Three Bar Ranch is the only competitor that borders my land and that's on the southwestern tip. We've never had an issue with them before."

Darcy picked up Adam's plate and walked it over to the sink. "You mentioned that Ralph inherits the ranch if you die, but does he not already own a percentage?"

"No," Adam replied. "Ralph is my stepbrother. After my mother died, my father engaged in reckless behavior and got a woman pregnant. The woman died when Ralph was seven, and he was dropped off at our doorstep."

"I imagine that came as a shock," Porter commented.

Adam nodded. "You could say that. The woman hadn't even informed my father she was pregnant."

"Does Ralph know?" Darcy asked over her shoulder as she washed the dishes.

"He does," Adam confirmed. "When my father's will was read, we learned that I had inherited the entire ranch, and Ralph was left with nothing."

Porter rose and grabbed a drying towel. As he reached for a wet plate, he asked, "How did Ralph handle the news?"

Adam leaned back in his seat. "He was only sixteen at the time our father passed, but he has never complained to me. Besides, Ralph is not behind this. I assure you."

"Why does Ralph not sleep in the house with you?" Darcy asked.

Adam shrugged. "He moved out after Amanda and I were married. He said that he wanted to give us privacy."

After he dried the plate, Porter placed it down on the counter. "Don't take offense that we consider Ralph a potential suspect. We have to consider all options before we clear someone."

Darcy extended him another plate to dry while she said, "I

will act the part of the housekeeper and clean, but I plan to join you when you ride out to that corner of the property."

"How exactly did you know I was planning to do that?" he asked, amused.

She flashed him a playful smile. "It appears that I can already anticipate your next move, *husband*."

"Perhaps I should ride with you both?" Adam asked, standing.

Porter reluctantly tore his gaze from Darcy's. "No, but a map would be helpful. You must be mindful to show me no favoritism. Treat me like you would any other hand."

"I hope you have thick skin," Adam joked. "I have high expectations for my cowhands."

"Good. As well as you should," Porter stated, placing the drying towel on the counter. "If you need to pass along a message, then slip into your house and inform Darcy."

"Understood," Adam replied, walking over to the door. "Shall we?"

Porter placed his hand on Darcy's waist, and he felt her stiffen. He leaned closer and whispered, "Stay safe, and don't take any unnecessary risks." He stepped back. "I will see you during my lunch break."

"I could say the same to you," she replied.

"Not necessary. I am a seasoned agent." He walked over to the hook next to the door and retrieved his Stenson. "Don't go anywhere without your gun."

Adam held open the door for him, but before he walked through it, Darcy said, "Thank you for helping with the dishes."

Placing the hat on his head, he tipped it towards her and headed out the door. Porter was pleased with himself. He was breaking down Darcy's barriers, and establishing trust between them. It had nothing to do with her alluring smile. He was learning more about her, so they could become more effective partners.

He sighed. He couldn't even convince himself that was true.

An Agent for Darcy

Chapter 5

Darcy looked around the parlor room with pride. All the dust had been removed, the walls were washed, windows scrubbed, carpets and drapes were brushed and shaken outside, and the floor swept. She reached down and picked up the water pail. On her way back to the kitchen, she grabbed the broom that was resting against the wall.

As she took her first step into the kitchen, the smell of the fire in the hearth and the combination of the stew brewing in the Dutch oven caused her to sigh in contentment. It had only taken her an hour to clean and dry the rest of the dishes and now the kitchen sparkled clean. She was immensely grateful for Porter's help. Josh had never once helped cleaned the dishes, claiming it was woman's work. However, her new husband didn't appear to have the same qualms about the tedious drudgery.

Porter was an interesting man, she thought to herself. He was devilishly handsome, and she found herself drawing closer to him. But no man could be as kind and considerate as he appeared to be. It must be an act for the sake of their assignment. After all, she was posing as a dutiful and loving wife, so it was only logical for him to act in a similar fashion. He was good though. He was so believable, that she had started falling for it.

Suddenly, the kitchen door was thrown open, and a tall cowboy, with a slender build and black hair sticking out from under his hat, stormed into the room.

"Adam!" He stopped when he saw her and quickly removed his Stetson. "Ma'am," he said, respectfully. "I apologize for barging in. By chance, have you seen my brother?"

"You must be Ralph," she stated as she dried her hands on her dress.

"Yes, ma'am," he replied. "I can't seem to find him outside, and I was hoping he came inside."

"I'm afraid not. I haven't seen him today." She walked over to the hearth, took the lid off the Dutch oven, and stirred the stew. "But I am expecting him for lunch. You are welcome to join us."

"That is a kind offer, but I eat with the other cowhands."

Darcy listened for any sign of resentment in his tone, but she found none. "Perhaps another time then."

"Did you find him?" a man's gruff voice came from behind Ralph.

"No, he's not in here," Ralph confirmed.

A man only a few inches taller than her, with a dark face, stern features, and a heavy brow, walked further into the room. His steps faltered when he saw her, and he quickly swiped his hat off his head. "I apologize, ma'am. We were trying to locate Mr. McCoy."

"I have been cleaning all morning, and I haven't heard him come home," she responded. "But I do expect him shortly."

The man's approving gaze roamed the kitchen. "You have done a remarkable job, Miss…" His words trailed off.

Ralph nudged the man in the stomach. "This is Mrs. Bailey, Adam's new housekeeper, and she is the wife of the new cowhand, Porter."

Disappointment flashed in the man's eyes, but he blinked it away. "It's a pleasure to meet you, Mrs. Bailey. My name is Dustin Weber."

"It is a pleasure to meet you both, Mr. Weber and Mr. McCoy," she acknowledged.

"We are not so familiar here at the ranch," Dustin remarked. "You must call me Dustin."

Ralph shifted in his stance. "And I go by Ralph here. Mr. McCoy is my brother."

Darcy waved her hand towards the Dutch oven. "There is plenty of stew if you'd like to join us."

"I am not sharing whatever that delightful smell is," Adam declared, walking into the room. Darcy heard a hint of humor in his words. "I've barely survived on that sludge that Don's been preparing for the cowhands."

Ralph grinned, his hands fidgeting with his hat. "You better not let Don hear you talking that way about his food."

Adam's eyes scanned the kitchen. "You have done a terrific job, Mrs. Bailey."

"Thank you," she responded. "Tomorrow is laundry day."

Letting out a sigh of relief, Adam said, "I can't tell you how pleased I am to hear that. I have been recycling clothes for far too long." He ignored the snickers from his cowhands as he pulled out a chair. "Why are you here in my home and not out working?" His tone was stern, but it held no bite.

"Dustin just informed me that I am not allowed to go out to the valley," Ralph declared in a frustrated tone.

"That's right," Adam confirmed. "But it's not just you. I have ordered that no one ventures that far until we sort this matter out."

Ralph let out a groan. "We have over two hundred cattle grazing in that field, including seventy-five of my own stock."

"It is not worth the risk," Adam contended.

"It may not be worth the risk to you," Ralph shouted, "but it is for me! My cattle are all that I own."

Adam frowned. "Be that as it may be, the cattle will be fine for a couple of weeks…"

Ralph stormed towards his brother, but Dustin placed his hand on Ralph's shoulder, holding him back. "If the cattle get lost in those mountain trails, we might never see them again," Ralph asserted. "I am going to check on my cattle."

"If you do, then you are fired," Adam stated firmly.

"Fired?" Ralph's mouth gaped open. "You would fire your own brother?"

"I would, and I will, if you do something foolish like putting your life on the line for something so inconsequential," Adam contended.

Ralph brushed off Dustin's hand. "You are a self-assured, uppity man and possess a head as hollow as a fiddle," he proclaimed. "Maybe you are making the cowhands disappear."

Adam shot up from his seat so fast that the chair fell to its side. "How dare you insinuate that I have anything to do with those men's disappearance."

Ralph stormed closer to his brother until they stood inches apart, his chest heaving with fury. "You have only ever cared about yourself," he growled.

"That is not true," Adam responded with a tightness in his voice. "I promised father that I would take care of *you*."

"By forcing me to live under your thumb," Ralph asserted

as he shoved his brother.

"Ralph, stop this," Dustin ordered, trying to step between the two men.

Adam came back swinging, hitting Ralph in the left eye, causing him to fumble backwards and knocking Dustin to the ground. Once Ralph regained his bearings, he reared his fist back and slammed it into Adam's stomach.

Tired of this useless altercation, Darcy took the derringer out of her pocket, pointed it towards the ceiling and fired a shot, resulting in white plaster dust filling the air. The men stopped fighting, and all stared at her in shock.

Returning the pistol to her pocket, Darcy gave them a stern look. "I do not allow fighting in my kitchen. If you would like to continue fighting, then please do so outside."

Ralph extended his hand to Dustin and helped him stand up. With mumbled apologies, Dustin and Ralph quickly left the house.

Darcy placed her hands on her hips and asked, "Do you want to explain what that was all about?"

Adam waved his hand dismissively. "It was nothing."

"Don't dismiss me." She lifted her brow. "Ralph clearly holds hostility towards you."

Adjusting his black vest, Adam replied, "He's just hot-headed."

"Apparently, so are you," Darcy huffed, dropping her hands.

"What in tarnation did you just say?" Adam asked in an annoyed tone.

Darcy rolled her eyes. "I don't think I could have made my statement simpler for you. You both have tempers, and you *both* escalated that fight."

Adam picked up his chair and sat down. "I am not paying you for your opinions, Mrs. Bailey," he drawled.

Moving to stand in front of him, Darcy crossed her arms over her chest. "But that is exactly what you are doing. What I just witnessed in this room is vital to our investigation." She watched as Adam's eyes narrowed disapprovingly. "Furthermore, if you ever say anything that insulting to me again," she paused, uncrossing her arms, "remember that I am a skilled nurse." Leaning closer, she whispered, "And I can make your death look like an accident."

Adam's eyes widened in disbelief as Darcy stepped back. "Now if you will excuse me, I am going to take a break. I find your presence to be unbearable at the moment."

Keeping her head held high, Darcy walked over to the door, opened it, and slammed it behind her.

Dusting off his trousers and shirt, Porter walked towards the house and saw Darcy sitting on a chair by the kitchen door. She was staring off into the distance. He wanted to shake his head at her lackadaisical attitude. A Pinkerton agent never had the luxury of being absentminded. They always had to be on guard.

As he hopped up the two steps onto the porch, he was about to open his mouth to give her his counsel, when she turned to face him. He saw the sadness in her eyes and immediately rushed to her side. "What's wrong?"

"Adam is not what he seems," she remarked.

He dropped to a knee in front of her. "Did he hurt you?" he asked, searching her body for injuries. His blood began to boil at the thought of Adam striking his wife. He would pay for this.

"No, no, no," she replied quickly. "Nothing like that. He just has a mean temper, as does his brother, Ralph."

"I haven't noticed that," Porter said, his anger cooling. "Both men gave orders but nothing that would indicate they had a quick fuse."

Darcy leaned closer to him, and she smelled like soap and sunshine, if that was even possible. "Ralph and Dustin came into the kitchen…" She shared the story of the altercation, and ended with, "I was so angry that I stormed outside."

Porter guffawed. "First of all, you can't threaten to kill our client. It's not written in the Pinkerton code, but it is an unwritten rule."

He watched her shoulders relax at his easy tone. "Now you tell me," she joked.

Reaching out, he brushed away the white plaster dust in her hair. "Do I even need to explain the dangers of discharging a pistol into the ceiling?"

"No," she murmured. "I figured that one out on my own."

He rose and offered his hand to assist her. "I am famished, and I only get a short break for my meal." Instead of releasing her hand right away, he held it as he walked to the kitchen door.

He stood aside as Darcy walked into the kitchen and saw Adam jump up from his chair at the table. "Mrs. Bailey, I want to apologize for my inappropriate remarks earlier." His words were rushed as he tried to ask for her forgiveness.

Darcy stood rigid, but she tilted her head in acknowledgement. Porter placed his hand on the small of her back. "Isn't there something you would like to say to Adam?"

She pressed her lips together for a moment before saying, "I am sorry for threatening to kill you."

Adam let out a bark of laughter. "I daresay I gave you reasonable cause." He pointed towards the chair. "Please sit and let's start over."

"Allow me to dish up bowls of stew first," Darcy said, taking a step towards the fireplace.

"Nonsense," Adam responded. "You sit, and I will serve you and your husband." He retrieved three bowls from the shelf and filled them full of piping hot stew.

Porter grabbed three spoons and walked back over to the table. He held out a chair for Darcy. "We have a few questions for you," he stated, directing his comment to Adam.

"I assumed as much," Adam acknowledged as he placed the bowls on the table.

Porter sat down next to Darcy. "You informed us that Ralph could not possibly be behind this, but Darcy witnessed your heated fight. Is it not conceivable that Ralph wants to ruin the McCoy Cattle Ranch?"

"For what purpose?" Adam asked, sitting down across from them. "If I go under, then he could lose everything as well."

"Ralph mentioned he owns cattle, and they are mingled with yours up in the valley," Darcy pointed out.

"It's true," Adam confirmed. "I gave him a hundred head of cattle last spring and they are branded with his own brand. Contrary to what you just witnessed, I do love my brother. I have even considered making him a part owner of the ranch, but he is too young for that type of responsibility. He is only twenty-one."

Porter took a bite of his stew, and his eyes grew wide. "This is fantastic stew!"

Darcy smiled at his praise. "You seem surprised."

"Why have I been cooking for you?" Porter joked. "Now that I know what a great cook you are, I demand you start making all of my meals."

She laughed as he hoped she would. "I should warn you that I can only make a few things well. Stew being one of them."

"I take it that you two are newlyweds," Adam observed, glancing between them. "How recent is it?"

"Typically, we don't discuss our personal lives with our clients," Porter informed him. "But, yes, it was recent."

"Oh, the bread," Darcy shouted, jumping up from her seat. "We can't have stew without bread."

As Darcy sliced the bread, Adam asked, "Are you still traveling to the north-west corner this evening?"

"Yes," Porter confirmed, his eyes lingering on Darcy.

"Good. I would like to go with you," Adam expressed.

Porter's eyes darted back towards him. "For what purpose?"

"I want to move the cattle to another pasture to ease Ralph's worry," Adam replied.

Darcy placed the bread on the table in front of him. "It might be dangerous for you."

Adam wore a solemn expression. "What exactly are you looking for?"

Porter shrugged one shoulder. "Anything that someone would be willing to kill for. We might be dealing with Indians or a crazy person that lives in the foothills. We won't know until we get up there."

"I have been racking my brain, but I have no idea why someone would want to kill my Amanda," Adam confessed. "Much less four cowhands. I have considered myself a fair employer, and I haven't fired anyone in years."

Porter pushed back his seat and rose. "Well, if you will excuse me, I need to get back to work. My boss is tough and doesn't allow slacking of any kind," he said, wiping his hand over his face to hide his growing smile.

Adam chuckled. "I'm sure the other men would understand if you were a few minutes late, because I'm sure they have seen your wife."

"I'm sure you're right. I married a beautiful woman," Porter admitted, enjoying the faint blush on Darcy's cheeks as she kept her gaze lowered. "I will be back after my shift, and we can take off shortly thereafter."

Adam rose. "I'll see to the horses."

"Darcy," Porter said, as he leaned closer to her ear, "stay out of trouble, *please*."

She tilted her head, causing their lips to be inches apart. "I can't make any promises," she jested with a cheeky smile on her lips.

His eyes became fixated on her lips. He had never had such a desire to kiss a woman as he did with Darcy.

Adam cleared his throat by the door. "If you are done memorizing your wife's features, we have work to get done."

Porter straightened and stepped back. "See you in a few hours," he mumbled as he followed Adam out the door.

Adam clapped him on the back. "You are a lucky, lucky man."

"I am," he responded, wishing, and not for the first time, that this was a real marriage.

An Agent for Darcy

Chapter 6

Reining in her horse, Darcy took a moment to admire the expansive green fields that sloped down towards the McCoy Cattle Ranch. The homestead looked so small, so inconsequential in the valley, especially compared to the imposing mountains looming behind her.

Kicking her horse into a run, she followed behind Porter and Adam as they rode higher and higher through the foothills until the Rocky Mountains started jutting up. Adam maneuvered them into a mountain pass and slowed their horses' gait to match the rocky terrain.

Darcy kept her alert eyes on the mountains on both sides of them. Tall pine trees loomed all around as they rode deeper into the mountains. The pass narrowed, forcing them to ride in single file. She was about to ask where they were going when they entered a wide valley filled with grazing cattle and bright flowers. A flowing river ran the length of the valley and disappeared back into the mountain terrain. This scene was picturesque.

"Now do you see why I am fighting so hard for this property?" Adam asked them as he surveyed his land with pride.

Darcy nodded. "I do. It is beautiful up here."

"Come. Let me show you the fence," Adam invited, urging his horse forward.

The cattle barely acknowledged them as they rode by, causing Darcy to smile. Lazy cattle. Near the far corner of the valley was a fence that spanned about fifty yards. Adam reined in his horse next to it. "This barrier prevents the cattle from going up this mountain path, which becomes steep and is quite treacherous."

Darcy's eyes roamed the valley, noting that except for this fence the entire valley was surrounded by rocky terrain that would be impossible for cattle to travel. "I see why you fenced off this area. This valley is the perfect place for grazing."

Porter dismounted his horse and secured it along the fence. "Is this where the horses of the missing cowhands were found?"

"It was," Adam confirmed as he dismounted. "There is no reason for my men to have gone past this fence or anywhere else in the mountains."

"Have you explored these hills, Adam?" she asked.

Adam shook his head. "I haven't had the time or the desire since I am much too busy trying to run a ranch. But my wife loved spending time in this valley. She enjoyed looking for caves."

Stepping behind the fence, Porter announced, "I am going to hike up this trail and see if I can find anything."

Darcy dismounted her horse and tied the lead to the fence. "Would you like me to go with you?"

"No, it is much too dangerous," Porter stated, over his shoulder. "I'll be back."

Darcy turned her eyes towards the imposing mountains and saw crevices in the rocks. If she was going to hide a body, tossing it into a crevice would be the perfect hiding place. She started hiking up the hill, climbing over huge, craggy rocks, and skirting the dense, dark green shrubbery that mingled with large pine trees that dotted the mountain landscape.

"I am not sure this is such a good idea," Adam said from somewhere behind her.

Darcy glanced over her shoulder. "If you're afraid, then you are welcome to turn back."

Not bothering to wait for his response, she continued to look around, hoping to find a clue. She had spent a considerable amount of time as a young girl looking for caves in the mountains that lined her family's ranch. Dark, enclosed spaces had never frightened her, much to her father's dismay.

That's when she saw it. An arched opening about twenty

yards up the hill, but it was partially hidden behind shrubbery. She hurried up the hill, barely able to contain her excitement. When she arrived at the thick bushes, she pushed them aside and saw a boulder blocking the lower portion of the entrance.

Darcy peered deep into the darkened cave, feeling an overwhelming desire to search this tunnel. However, this was not a pleasure trip. She was looking for clues that would help them find the missing cowhands. "Doesn't it seem odd that a boulder is blocking the entrance into this cave?"

"Not particularly," Adam admitted.

Her eyes roamed the dirt surrounding the shrubbery, noting the unusually smooth ground, but she also noticed small overturned pebbles. To confirm her theory, she saw that some of the low growing plants had been broken off. "It appears that someone wiped away their tracks but wasn't careful when they stepped on the plants."

"Why would someone go through the trouble of wiping away their tracks up here?"

"Exactly. What is that person hiding?" Darcy put her hands on the boulder and futilely tried to shove it away.

"Allow me to help you," Adam said, reaching around her and rolling the boulder to the side.

"Thank you," she murmured, dusting her hands off on the skirt of her dress.

She ducked her head down and stepped into the darkened cave. She heard the sound of dripping water in the distance, and the air was damp and cool. "You don't have a lantern by chance, do you?" she asked, knowing that Adam was right behind her.

"Unfortunately, I left my lantern in my other vest pocket," he replied sarcastically.

Darcy ignored his cheeky response and stepped further into the cave. The only light streamed in from the opening and a blanket of darkness loomed ahead of her. Not deterred by the lack of light, she started walking down the tunnel.

Adam grabbed her arm from behind, causing her to gasp. "You can't just walk into a cave without light. You could plummet to your death if you're not careful."

Reluctantly, she knew he had a point. "We'll need to come back with a lantern."

She backtracked her steps and exited the cave. After they shoved the boulder back into place, Darcy kept her eyes trained for any other caves or crevices that were wide enough to hide a body.

"Darcy!" Porter's frantic voice echoed off the mountain walls. "Darcy!"

"Coming!" Darcy hurried down the terrain, not realizing how far she had gone in her initial search of the crevices. When she broke through the trees, she could see Porter held his revolver in his hand. "What's wrong?"

Porter gave her an exasperated look before he tucked his pistol back into his gun belt. "Where in the blazes have you been?"

"Searching," Darcy revealed as she heard Adam come to a stop behind her. "We found the most unusual cave..." She stopped speaking when she saw Porter glaring at her. "What is it?"

Porter pointed towards the path she had just come down. "You can't just wander around these hills alone."

Adam cleared his throat. "This might be a bad time to point out that I was with her, so she wasn't *alone*."

Ignoring Adam, Porter marched up to her. "Need I remind you that four disappearances have happened in this valley. *Four*."

"I am well aware of that fact, considering that's what we came out here to investigate." Darcy lifted her brow. "May I point out that *you* just wandered off on *your* own?"

"That's different!" Porter exclaimed.

"In what way?" she countered.

Porter huffed. "I don't require *your* protection, but you do require mine."

"I beg your pardon?"

He grabbed her elbow and led her away from Adam's prying ears. "You are a woman, and an untrained agent. You are not to chase down a lead without first obtaining my approval. Do I make myself clear?"

Darcy reared back in disbelief. Porter didn't consider her a partner, or his equal. He only considered her as someone he had to protect, and no matter what she did, she recognized that it wouldn't change his mind. "You are supposed to be my partner. I never asked you to be my protector."

"We will discuss this later," Porter declared, his eyes darting towards Adam.

Ignoring her dolt of a husband, Darcy directed her next question towards Adam. "Do you require my assistance in relocating the cattle?"

"No," Adam replied with a shake of his head.

"Just as I assumed." She brushed past Porter and mounted her horse. "I will see you back at the cottage."

As she road off, she heard Porter shout, "Darcy, get back here!"

Never. Porter had humiliated her in front of Adam. For a short time, she had thought he was different. But she was wrong. He had been manipulating her, controlling her. Never again.

She would never be controlled by another man... trainer, or

no trainer.

Darcy hummed as she picked up the cookies from the cooling rack and placed them into the basket. On the ride home, she decided that she would prove her worth to Porter by solving the case on her own. But the only lead they had was that cave, and it might not even be related to the case.

She was tired of sitting inside, waiting for something to happen. She was going to seek out the information from the potential suspects themselves. The cowhands. Her plan was to loosen their tongues with cookies.

As she walked towards the bunkhouse, the sun was dipping below the horizon, and the fleeting colors of dusk began to fade away. She stopped in front of the crude wood building and knocked on the door. The door was wrenched open and Dustin, wearing only his trousers and no shirt, stood in front of her.

"Mrs. Bailey," Dustin cried out before he lunged out of view. A moment later, he was wearing a shirt and tried again. "I wasn't expecting it to be you, ma'am."

Darcy smiled. "I made some cookies, and I thought you gentlemen would like some."

"Gentlemen." A deep grunt came from inside the room. "You got the wrong bunkhouse."

"Well, if you aren't interested…" she said, letting her words trail off.

"Not at all," Dustin replied, holding his hand out.

Rather than extend him the basket, she brushed past him into the communal home with beds lining the walls. A wood stove sat in the center of the room with drying poles running the length of the structure. Socks, shirts, and other garments were hanging from these poles. The cowhands were playing cards around a table near the stove.

Dustin cleared his throat, and all the men in the room jumped up from their seats. In a coordinated effort, the cowboys all grabbed their garments off the drying poles and tossed them onto their beds.

"I am sorry to barge in on you gentlemen," Darcy started, "but Porter and Mr. McCoy aren't back from relocating the cattle from the north-west corner."

"When did my brother decide to do that?" Ralph asked from his seat.

Darcy walked further into the room and placed the basket on the table. "After you left, Mr. McCoy decided to relocate the cattle since he knew how much they meant to you."

An older man with silver hair sat next to the stove, stirring the contents of a large iron pot. "That would be a first," he mumbled under his breath. That had to be Don, the cook, she thought.

Dustin walked over to his bed and dropped down. "Let's hope that Adam has come to his senses and builds a fence to block off that valley."

Ralph sighed. "No way Adam will do that. He loves that valley too much," he hesitated, "as did Amanda."

"Four men have disappeared and are most likely dead. I don't care about that good-for-nothing valley," a dark-haired cowboy interjected.

"I have no doubt that someone ambushed those men," the cook said. "I'm telling you, it's those Indians doing the killing."

"The Indians have never been hostile towards us before," Ralph contested.

The man removed the ladle from the soup and pointed it at him. "The only good Indian is a dead Indian."

Ralph rolled his eyes as he rose from his seat and directed his next comment towards her. "I apologize for Don's backwards thinking. He was dropped on his head as a child."

Don grunted. "No. I just speak the truth."

"Diluted truth," Dustin corrected.

Darcy's eyes scanned the group of worn, rough-looking men and said, "I'm afraid I haven't had the opportunity to meet most of you. My name is Mrs. Darcy Bailey."

"We know who you are, ma'am," the dark-haired man replied. "My name is Tom."

Darcy tipped her head graciously. "It is a pleasure to meet you, Tom."

Tom provided the rest of the introductions. "You already met Dustin, Ralph, and everyone knows Don." He pointed towards a brawny man with a blue bandana around his neck. "That's John."

With a suave smile on his lips, John tipped his head towards her. "Ma'am. It is always a pleasure to meet such a beautiful woman."

A stodgy man next to John swatted at him with the cards in his hands. "She is married, you ninny. Save your charms for another sucker." He met her gaze. "My name is Bill," he pointed towards the man next to him, "and this here's my brother, Butch."

In the corner, a tall man with wide shoulders leaned back against the wall. "My name is Perry," he said in a grizzly tone.

Darcy gave the group a tentative smile. "It's nice to meet all of you. I apologize for barging in on you, but I am not used to being alone at night."

"Would you like to sit for a spell, ma'am?" Ralph asked, picking up his chair and repositioning it next to her.

"Thank you, Ralph," she murmured, gracefully sitting

down. She took the basket and removed the linen napkin, revealing a pile of cookies. "Please, help yourselves."

The men all lunged forward, and Darcy feared that they would break out into a fight. Don banged the ladle against the side of the pot. "Have you all forgot your manners, you worthless lot?" He grabbed the basket and yanked it towards him. "I will hand out a cookie to each one of you."

While Don passed out the cookies, she attempted to make her next words sound casual. "Mr. McCoy informed me that he employs almost twenty cowhands. Where are the others?"

Ralph nodded. "That's right, but us cowhands take turns sleeping out on the range during the warm months to prevent cattle rustlin'."

"I see." Darcy decided to attempt another conversation about the valley. "I must admit that I was nervous when Porter informed me that he was going with Mr. McCoy to move the cattle out of the valley. I have been praying for their safe return."

Dustin sat back down on his bed and leaned his back up against the wall. "In my opinion, we need to stay far away from that valley."

"Is there a reason why Mr. McCoy refuses to take your advice?" she asked innocently.

"Because my brother is a stubborn fool," Ralph spoke up.

"He has plenty of grazing land, but he refuses to leave that valley, even temporarily."

Tom shoved the cookie in his mouth before saying, "If he doesn't rotate through that land then some other cattle rancher could claim that valley."

"Doesn't he own the land?" she questioned.

"Ownership is a funny thing in the west," Dustin remarked. "It is easier to maintain ownership if one has possession of something, and the McCoys never bought the land. They staked out a squatter's claim."

"Do you think someone is trying to kick him out of the valley?" Darcy asked.

Pushing off from the wall, Perry asserted, "That is exactly what someone is trying to do."

Darcy accepted the empty basket back from Don with a smile. "For what purpose?"

Perry shrugged. "Grazing rights, waterhole… who knows."

"I think it is because of gold," Tom spoke up in an excited tone.

Dustin let out an annoyed groan. "Here we go again."

Tom leaned forward in his seat and explained, "Multiple mother loads of gold have been found throughout the Rocky Mountains. The streams are filled with gold nuggets."

"I have yet to see a stream filled with gold nuggets," Perry joked.

"You can deny it, but it would make sense," Tom said, not deterred by Perry's teasing comment. "I think a prospector is in those hills and is killing anyone that steps foot in the valley."

Darcy gasped, bringing her hand up to cover her mouth. "You don't think Porter will be shot for helping Mr. McCoy?" she asked, her tentative voice barely above a whisper.

Ralph tossed a shirt at Tom, hitting him on the head. "Will you stop flapping your trap? You're scaring Mrs. Bailey."

Tom removed the shirt and dropped it on the ground. "I am sure Porter is fine," he stated in a reassuring tone.

Now that she discovered the information she had hoped to obtain, Darcy rose from her seat. "I suppose I should be heading back to my cottage," she murmured.

"Are you familiar with the game 'jackpots'?" Bill asked, holding up a deck of cards.

A genuine smile came to Darcy's lips. "It's my favorite card game."

"You are full of surprises, Mrs. Bailey," Dustin acknowledged, pulling his bed frame closer to the wood stove.

You have no idea, she thought, accepting the cards that Bill dealt.

Chapter 7

Porter stormed out of the stable. He couldn't recall a time when he had been angrier than he was right now. Not only had Darcy carelessly been searching the caves, but she had disobeyed him when she had ridden home alone. What was that woman thinking? Did she not have a lick of sense? A murderer was loose in those hills, and she just up and left when he had reprimanded her.

He was the lead partner. Darcy was an untrained agent. Why did she discount what he said so easily? She was completely aware that he couldn't leave Adam to relocate those cattle alone. She had intentionally fled from him.

The sun had set before Adam and Porter arrived back at the stable. Even though he wanted to rail at Darcy the moment he got back, he needed to see that his horse was brushed, fed, and put away for the evening.

Adam's voice broke him out of his thoughts. "Porter!" he barked from behind him.

Porter stopped and spun back around. "Yes."

"You might want to go easy on your wife."

"Is that so?" he asked, crossing his arms in front of his chest. "Why is that?"

Not appearing intimidated by his bristly tone, Adam closed the distance between them. "You were unfair to her in the valley."

"Unfair? In what way?"

Adam furrowed his brows, and he lowered his voice. "May I offer some advice?"

"You may."

"You were completely justified in your anger but try to look at it from your wife's perspective," Adam shared.

"Darcy could have gotten herself killed," he pointed out, uncrossing his arms.

"True, but she didn't," Adam said, giving him a knowing look. "Furthermore, she didn't get reckless until after *you* berated her."

"I didn't berate her," he contended, "I was training her."

Adam wore a look of confusion. "You were training her for what?"

He removed his hat and hit it against the side of his trousers. "Darcy is a new agent, and as her husband, I have been assigned to train her."

Adam chuckled. "I wish you luck with that, but I find that wives don't like to be bossed around so much." He gave him a pointed look. "If Darcy kicks you out, you are welcome to stay in one of my guest rooms."

"Thank you, but that won't be necessary," Porter replied confidently.

He was still fuming as he made the short trek to his cottage, but as he got closer, he realized that no light came from within. It was completely dark.

Increasing his stride, he rushed to open the door, but was met with the deafening sound of silence. "Darcy!" He ran straight down the hall and opened the door to her room. His heart dropped when he saw it was empty. His next step was to run into the kitchen, but nothing was out of place.

Porter fell back against the wall. His anger quickly melted away, and it was replaced with a sense of panic. Did Darcy leave? Did she abandon him? Straightening up, he ran back into her bedroom and saw that her trunk was still there. Wherever she went, it hadn't been far. He snapped his fingers as an idea struck him. The house.

Porter sprinted towards Adam's home. Without bothering to knock, he tossed open the kitchen door.

Adam jumped up from his chair. "What is it?" he cried out,

alarmed.

"Darcy is gone. Is she here?" he asked as he ran through the kitchen and into the parlor. Running up the stairs, he checked each room, but he found no trace of her.

"Did you find her?" Adam asked from the base of the stairs.

"No!" he exclaimed. "Where could she be?"

"We saw her horse in the stall," Adam reminded him. "Which means, wherever she went, she walked."

"It is dark outside. Why isn't she in the safety of the cottage?" he asked, frantically. What was happening to him? He was a Pinkerton agent. He never got frazzled. But the thought of Darcy being hurt caused him to shake to his very core. She was his partner, his responsibility... his wife.

Adam walked over towards the door. "Before you start panicking, I propose we go speak to the cowhands. They might know something."

Porter nodded as he followed Adam out the door, but his mind was whirling with the possibilities. What if Darcy had been abducted? If so, he should be out looking for her. What if she had been ambushed on the way back to the homestead and the murderer had returned her horse to avoid suspicion?

Before he knew it, they had arrived at the bunkhouse. Adam took his fist and pounded on the door. A smiling Ralph opened the door, but his smile dimmed when he saw their hardened faces. "Is everything okay?"

"Mrs. Bailey is missing," Adam informed his brother.

"No, she ain't," Ralph replied, opening the door wide. "She is playing cards with us."

"What?" Porter shouted, storming into the room.

Darcy was sitting around a table with the cowhands, holding cards in her hand. When she looked up at him, her smile vanished for a moment, before a forced smile came to her lips. "You're finally home," she said in what sounded like a cheery voice. But Porter detected the anger behind her words.

"I came home to an empty cottage, and I was worried about you," he said, honestly.

Her eyes trailed over the cowhands. "These gentlemen have been kind enough to keep me company while you were out."

The cowboys all watched her with enamored looks on their faces. It was clear that many of these men found her company to be more than tolerable. Porter clenched his jaw so tight that he started grinding his teeth. What was she thinking, keeping company with these men?

Darcy rose, but not before she turned over her cards. "I believe I will leave on a high note."

A few of the cowhands leaned forward and stared at her cards in disbelief. "You won again? Who taught you how to play?" Tom asked, wiping his hand over his chin.

"The cowhands at my father's ranch taught me," she admitted.

"They did a right fine job," stated a gruff older man by the stove.

Porter tipped his Stetson at the cowboys. "See you all tomorrow," he said as Darcy came to stand next to him.

"Good night, and thank you for a wonderful evening," Darcy acknowledged with a smile.

Adam stepped next to the chair that Darcy had departed and asked, "Mind if I join you for a few hands?"

"Don't mind if you do," Dustin declared, "but our boss is a real slave driver. We shouldn't stay up much later."

Adam laughed as he sat down.

Offering his arm to Darcy, Porter was pleased when she accepted it. They walked out the door, but she dropped her hand as soon as the door closed behind them. The rest of the walk back to their cottage she looked everywhere but at him. He would have given all that he had to get her to acknowledge him.

When they arrived at their door, he held it open and stood aside as she walked into the dark cottage. He stepped through, closing the door behind him. Darcy went over to the lantern in the kitchen, and he followed closely behind her.

As soon as the lantern was lit, Porter grabbed her by the waist and pulled her tight against him.

It would have been proper of her to resist being in Porter's arms, but Darcy didn't feel like being proper. His warm embrace made her feel safe and protected, something she hadn't felt in a long time. She laid her head against his chest and could feel his heartbeat through his layers of clothing.

She closed her eyes as she relished this moment. Her ruggedly handsome husband was not truly hers, and this intimate position was entirely inappropriate. But why did it feel so right?

After a long moment, Porter leaned back, but he didn't release her from his arms. "I thought you had left."

"Left where?"

He sighed. "I don't know. I came home to a darkened cottage, and I just," he hesitated, "I got scared."

Unsure of his meaning, she asked, "Scared about what?"

He dropped his arms from around her waist and brought them up to cup her face. "I thought you left me, and it petrified me."

"Oh, Porter," she whispered. "I wouldn't have left without saying goodbye."

Frown lines appeared next to his lips. "You have thought about leaving?"

She gave him a perplexed look. "Of course, I have. We are not truly married. After this case, we will get an annulment and go our separate ways."

Scoffing, Porter dropped his hands and stepped back. "How silly of me. You are correct." His words were devoid of emotion.

"Isn't that what you want?"

Porter shifted his gaze over her shoulder. "At the beginning, yes. But now…" His words stilled as his eyes roamed her face. "I have spoken out of turn. This is not the time to discuss such things."

She pulled out a chair at the table and sat down. "I agree. We are in the middle of a case."

"No, you are in the process of trying to get yourself killed with your outlandish actions," Porter growled.

Her expression turned determined. "No man has the right to control me," she paused, "and that includes you."

Porter reached for a chair and yanked it back. "I am your trainer. My job is to ensure you don't get yourself killed."

"That stunt back in the valley was not you trying to train me," Darcy informed him. "That was you trying to control me."

Leaning his forearms on the table, Porter declared, "There is a murderer loose in those hills and you were just traipsing…"

She let out an exasperated sigh. "I was not traipsing. I thought to myself that a cave would be a fantastic place to hide a body, and I went in search of any opening."

"You are going to be the death of me, Darcy Shaw," Porter stated. "Where do you think a murderer would hide? Out in the open?" He shook his head. "No, he would hide in a cave."

Even though she was secretly pleased that he called her Darcy Shaw, she could not let him get the upper hand. "Adam was with me, and I was carrying a derringer."

"Forgive me," Porter drawled, "I was mistaken. You *obviously* were not being lax about your safety."

Darcy frowned. "Has anyone ever told you that you are infuriatingly annoying?"

"No. Quite the opposite, in fact."

"Who told you that? Your mother?" Darcy quipped.

"You are awful at insults." A hint of a smile played on his lips before it disappeared. "Regardless, you should have waited for me to accompany you in your search of the caves."

"Why?" she asked defiantly.

He furrowed his brows. "I believe I already explained…"

"Admit it. You don't think I will ever be as good of an agent as you are," Darcy declared, rising.

Leaning back in his seat, Porter pressed his lips together.

"Women and men have different strengths…"

Darcy spoke over him, "Don't patronize me with your rationalization."

She turned to walk out of the room, but Porter reached out and grabbed her hand. "You must understand that women think with their emotions, and that is a dangerous way to solve a case."

"Good night, Porter," she said, yanking back her hand.

"Wait," Porter responded, rising. "At least tell me what you discovered in the mountains."

Darcy reluctantly sat back down in her seat. As she shared her discovery, she grew excited. "We found an opening with a boulder positioned in front of it, and someone had taken the time to wipe away their tracks."

"That's odd," he murmured. "How did you know that someone had wiped their tracks?"

She pursed her lips. "Is it so unbelievable that a woman can be good at tracking?"

"No," he replied. "I am just… impressed."

Ignoring his backhanded comment, she revealed, "I also went to the bunkhouse tonight with a specific purpose." Porter opened his mouth, most likely to say something insulting, so she pressed forward. "The cowhands are adamant that someone is attempting to force Adam from the valley."

Porter gave her a look that was a mixture of frustration and sympathy. "We already knew that."

"True, but Tom thinks it's because there's gold in those mountains." She smiled victoriously.

"Gold?" He frowned. "You can't be serious."

"Perfectly. Why else would someone go to such great lengths to remove Adam from the valley?"

Porter put his hands up in front of him. "It is a picturesque valley. I am sure there are countless other reasons someone would want to lay claim to the land."

Darcy placed her hands on her hips. "At least I *have* a lead."

"I hate to break it to you, but gold in the mountains is not a lead. It is a wild goose chase," he huffed.

"You're impossible!" she exclaimed. "I'm going to bed. I just hope you aren't such a blockhead when I wake up."

"Name calling?" He removed his hat and went to place it on a hook. "I didn't think you would resort to such childishness."

Darcy refused to dignify his comment with a response. She walked down the hall and entered her room. To emphasize how mad she was at Porter, she slammed the door shut.

No matter what she did, Porter would never take her seriously as an agent. How could she get him to change his mind?

Tears came to her eyes, but she quickly blinked them away. She had learned a long time ago that crying resolved nothing. It was just a sign of weakness, and she refused to cry over Porter Shaw.

Chapter 8

Porter stood outside Darcy's door. It had been hours since she'd stormed off and slammed it behind her. He had tried to fall asleep on his pad on the ground near the fireplace, but he couldn't get the look of Darcy's wounded expression out of his mind. He hadn't meant to hurt her when he explained why women agents could never be as good as their male counterparts. There were exceptions, of course, most notably, Mrs. Kate Warne.

The more he dwelt on it, the more he realized that the gold angle might be the break in the case that they needed. It did make sense, because gold lust could make any sane man go crazy. Besides, men have killed for a lot less in the Wild West.

Now he was standing outside of Darcy's door, debating whether he should knock. She was probably asleep. He should go lay back down. However, he doubted that he would be able to sleep tonight if he didn't apologize to her first.

Lifting his hand, he rapped his knuckles against the door.

"Come in," Darcy responded immediately.

He placed his hand on the handle and opened the door. "It isn't locked," he stated in surprise.

"No. I have no reason to fear you." She sat up in her bed and rested her back against the wall.

Her admission secretly pleased him. Porter leaned his shoulder against the door frame. "I came to apologize for my behavior earlier."

"That's kind of you," Darcy said, her fingers toying with the high neck of her nightgown. "I would also like to apologize for my behavior."

"You did nothing wrong."

Her eyes snapped up to his. "We both know that's not true."

With a smirk on his lips, he replied, "I will accept your apology only because you wounded me with your vulgar talk."

"Vulgar talk?"

"When you called me a," he paused, lowering his voice, " '*blockhead*'."

She let out a small laugh. "There is something about you that just irks me sometimes."

"Is it because I am so incredibly handsome?"

"No, that's not it," she said, but her response seemed forced.

"Charming?"

Darcy rolled her eyes. "You clearly do not lack in the humility department."

He brought his hand up to his chest, feigning hurt. "Why are you so cruel to me?"

She laughed, and it warmed his heart. "I don't know how you always manage to cheer me up," she remarked.

Porter grinned. "That is the job of a good husband." Her countenance dimmed at his words, and he felt like kicking himself for the insensitive comment. "I'm sorry... I wasn't thinking..."

She lowered her eyes to the quilt. "You have no reason to apologize. What you said was accurate."

"You mentioned before that Josh died in a shoot-out, but what were the circumstances around his death?" he asked, hoping he hadn't overstepped his bounds.

Her eyes met his, and he saw a deep sorrow lurking behind them. "It's painful to speak about," she murmured.

Porter stepped further into the room and sat down on a chair next to the bed. "I have all night."

Darcy started fidgeting with the lace at the end of her sleeves, and it was a long moment before she began her story. "During the day, it was common for Josh to be called out to someone's home for an emergency. He always insisted I stayed behind to run the clinic, and to see to the needs of his other patients. He would be gone for hours, sometimes even all night." She pressed her lips tightly together. "I was aware that he would stop at the saloon for drinks, but I had no idea that he was a regular at a brothel in the red district."

Porter lifted his brow. He hadn't expected that. "A brothel?"

"Yes," she confirmed. "From what I gathered after his death, he went to the brothel almost daily and spent the majority of his time with a girl named Sadie." Her tone grew hollow. "Josh had proposed to Sadie, and she had accepted. The only issue was that he was still married to me."

Afraid of where this was going, Porter just stayed quiet, unsure of what words could even provide her comfort.

"Uh... together, they hatched a plan to kill me and were days away from committing the murder," she revealed reluctantly.

His mouth gaped open. "What happened?"

She closed her eyes for a moment. "One of the other girls overheard the plot and informed the sheriff. When he went to question Josh and Sadie, Josh pulled his pistol and shot the sheriff right in front of the patrons at the brothel. Fortunately, he didn't kill the sheriff, and a shoot-out occurred." Tears formed in her eyes, but she blinked them back vigorously. "Ten people were killed in the brothel that day, including Josh and Sadie."

Porter moved to sit on the bed. "That must have been horrible for you."

Frown lines appeared between her eyebrows. "When I heard the shooting, I grabbed my bag and I ran over to the brothel to provide medical care to the victims. I had no idea that my husband was responsible…" Her voice cracked with emotion. "How could he do such a thing… to the town… to me?"

Unable to resist, he reached out and pulled her into a tight embrace. "I am so sorry that happened to you."

Darcy molded against him and brought her arms around his waist. "To make it worse, the moment Josh's body was buried, I started receiving marriage proposals."

He rested his chin on the top of her head. "That's odd."

"Where I lived, a single woman was a rare commodity, and men came from all over to offer for me."

"How many offers did you receive?" he asked curiously.

"Over a hundred."

He huffed. "You can't be serious."

"Sadly, I am," she confirmed. "In addition to being a woman, I am also a part owner of a successful cattle ranch."

"And a nurse."

He felt her shake her head. "That meant little to some of the men."

"I am so sorry your husband was such a despicable cad, and the men in your town were so insensitive…" His words stilled as his anger built inside of him at the pain that Josh and the menfolk caused her. "I promise that no one will ever hurt you again," he vowed, knowing he would risk his own life to protect this woman.

"Thank you," she whispered, "but right now, will you just hold me?"

He kissed the top of her head. "Anything for you, darling."

As he continued to hold her in his arms, Porter recognized that he had never felt this way about a woman before. Darcy held a familiarity that he could not seem to explain. It was as if they belonged together. And he was becoming fairly certain that they *did* belong together.

Darcy did not trust easily. He would need to proceed with caution and start courting her slowly.

As Darcy swept the kitchen floor in Adam's house, her mind kept wandering to Porter. He was an anomaly. Every time she saw him, her heart would practically leap from her chest, as if recognizing that it had found a safe haven with him. Which was preposterous.

Porter was her partner, and husband in name only. So why

did the thought of getting an annulment cause her stomach to ache? Josh had never been as kind and loving as Porter, but he had started off as a decent human being. She had been fooled by his handsome face and charisma. And what had it got her? Embarrassment and shame. Never again, she told herself.

She sighed as she stopped sweeping. Porter had left a kind note on her pillow this morning and even made her a bowl of oatmeal before he left for his shift. Earlier, he had stopped by the kitchen as she was peeling potatoes and brought her flowers. He even spent his lunch break helping her with the potatoes.

What did he hope to achieve with all those flowery words and acts of kindness? Men rarely did something just to be kind. Although, that was not a fair statement. Her brother and father were good men, as were a decent amount of men in her town. She just didn't want to risk being deceived again. She was scared.

"That is one serious look," Adam said, removing his hat and placing it on the hook by the door.

Darcy blinked over at him in surprise. "I didn't even hear you come in."

"I reckoned that was the case," he replied. "Is everything all right?"

"Perfectly."

He let out an amused huff. "For being a Pinkerton agent,

you are not very good at lying."

Ignoring his comment, she returned the broom to the corner and asked, "Are you hungry? Supper is almost ready."

"I sure am." Adam walked over and sat down at the table. "I must admit, I'll be sad once you and Porter solve this case."

"Is that so?" she asked, lifting the pot and stirring the contents.

"It's been nice to have someone to talk to again."

Darcy looked over at him in surprise. "You have a brother and more than twenty cowhands working here."

He gave her a wistful smile. "It is not the same as a wife."

Wiping her hands off on her apron, she gave him an understanding nod. "It is especially hard for the first few months, but I must warn you that the grieving period never stops. Although, one day you will wake up, and it will hurt a little less."

Adam watched her intently. "You seem to speak from experience."

"My dad died a little over a year ago and," she hesitated, attempting to find the strength, "I was married before Porter."

"I am sorry for both of your losses."

Uncomfortable with his sympathy, she dismissed his comment with a wave of her hand. "My father and Josh both died unexpectedly."

"Much like Amanda," he murmured.

"No, nothing like Amanda," she admitted. "My father died while out on a cattle run and as for Josh…" She looked up at the ceiling. "He was not a good man."

"Did he hurt you?" Adam asked in a concerned voice.

She brought her gaze down to meet his. "Let's just say that I am not sad that he is gone."

"It is a good thing you found Porter then."

A twinge of guilt came over her. It was a good thing she found Porter, but he was not hers to keep. Even though he was teaching her how a man should treat his wife, with love and acts of kindness, he would go away after they got an annulment. Realizing that Adam was still waiting for a reply, she mumbled, "Very lucky."

Adam let out a deep, heartfelt sigh. "I have been so lost these past few weeks without Amanda. How do I find the strength to move on?"

Darcy sat down next to him. "You pick up the pieces of your shattered heart, one by one, until it is strong enough for you to start over."

Tears came to his eyes. "I don't think I can. I still smell Amanda's scent on her pillow and the pain becomes overwhelming."

When a tear leaked out of his eyes, she reached over and placed her hand on his sleeve. "That is because you loved her dearly, without any restraints. She was lucky to have you."

His lips pressed firmly together before admitting, "She wasn't happy here, you know. She didn't enjoy being a rancher's wife."

"It can be quite lonely for a woman to live on a cattle ranch," Darcy expressed. "You're far from town and surrounded by men."

Adam stared at her, his eyes filled with pain and regret. "It was because of me that Amanda is dead and four of my employees… my friends." He scoffed. "For what? A piece of land?"

"You did nothing wrong. This is not your fault."

He dropped his head in his hands. "What have I done?"

"Don't give up. You owe that to Amanda," Darcy replied reassuringly as she leaned closer. "You must fight through the grief and the guilt."

"Why?" he asked, lifting his head.

Compassion grew inside of her since she understood exactly what he was going through. "Fight for yourself, because it will get better. Trust me."

He watched her, his expression hopeful. "How is that possible when I don't have Amanda with me?"

Darcy gave him an understanding smile. "When you truly love someone, they will always be a part of you."

"Do you honestly believe that?" he murmured earnestly.

"I do, wholeheartedly."

The kitchen door slammed closed and Porter's deep voice rang out. "Pardon me. Did I interrupt something just now?" he asked, his voice taking on a hard edge.

Darcy straightened and stood up. "Nope. Supper is ready." She smiled over at Porter. "How was your afternoon?"

Porter tore his narrowed gaze away from Adam, and his eyes softened when they landed on her. "It went well. I spent some time calf roping."

She grabbed two plates and filled them with generous helpings of beef, potatoes and vegetables. She walked over and placed them in front of the men. "Eat up. I found preserved vegetables. I assume your wife canned them. Am I right?"

Adam reached for his fork. "You are correct."

After she filled her plate, she sat down next to Porter. She hadn't even taken her first bite when he said, "I've decided that we need to set a trap."

An Agent for Darcy

Chapter 9

Porter watched as Darcy gave him her full attention. "As much as I enjoy being a cowhand, it's time we set a trap for the murderer."

"How do you propose we do that?" Darcy asked.

He pointed his fork at Adam. "You are going to assign me to go mend the fence in the valley. If all goes well, we can lure out the murderer and arrest him before supper tomorrow."

"But why would I send you and not Dustin, who is the acting foreman?" Adam questioned.

Porter shrugged. "You're the boss. Think of a reason."

"What happens after you lure the criminal into the valley?" Darcy inquired.

After he swallowed his food, he replied, "I'll be waiting for him."

Darcy looked expectantly at him. "And where do I fit into this plan?"

"You will stay behind," Porter replied, his tone brooking no argument.

"Absolutely not," she declared, her voice rising. "I'm going with you."

Since he expected her outburst, he was unperturbed. "It won't be safe for you."

"Fine," she replied quickly. Much too quickly.

Porter had not expected that. He had anticipated more of a fight. He eyed her suspiciously. It was clear that she was up to something, but he couldn't figure out what it was.

Seeming oblivious to his scrutiny, Darcy smiled sweetly at Adam. "How was your day today?"

He wiped his mouth with his napkin and answered, "It was…"

Porter spun in his chair to face Darcy and spoke over Adam. "I am serious. You cannot come with me."

With a mischievous glint in her eye, she acknowledged, "I understand." She turned her gaze back to Adam for him to finish.

Adam's eyes darted between them. "Um… as I was saying…"

"Fine. You can come!" he exclaimed, pointing his finger at her. "But you will stay hidden."

Her lips twitched but the rest of her face was expressionless. "I don't accept your terms." She lifted her brow at Adam. "Please continue."

Adam leaned back in his seat with amusement on his features. "Why don't I wait until you two finish…" he paused, smirking, "whatever this is?"

"Darcy," Porter said, "you must understand that we are trying to trap a murderer."

"I understand. That is why I signed up to be a Lady Pinkerton."

As a seasoned agent, he had learned to read people with remarkable accuracy. However, Darcy was different. Sometimes he could read her like an open book, and other times she hid her emotions behind a mask. It was maddening. His instincts were telling him that he would not win this argument with his wife.

"What do you propose?" he asked through gritted teeth.

She pressed her brow together in concentration. "I propose that we leave immediately and tour that cave. With any luck, it will give us a clue to why someone is willing to kill to keep it hidden."

Drats! That was actually a good idea. "All right," he agreed, wiping his mouth with his linen napkin and tossing it onto the table. "Let's ride."

Adam rose from his seat. "Would you like me to join you?"

"No," Porter responded, a little too quickly, "I want my wife all to myself." He stopped, realizing what he had just revealed. It was true. He wanted to spend time alone with Darcy, and he doubted he would ever tire of her smile, or their banter.

"Fair enough," Adam said. "I'll go prepare your horses and bring them around back."

"I'll get two lanterns," Darcy informed them as she walked out of the room.

Porter glanced over his shoulder before lowering his voice. "If I don't make it back for work tomorrow…" His words died off, hoping that Adam caught his meaning.

Adam nodded. "Be safe. For your wife's sake."

Darcy walked back into the room holding two black lanterns. "You ready?"

Unable to help himself, he walked up to her and kissed her on the right cheek. "Are you ready to see the glamorous life of an agent?"

He was pleased to see a blush staining her cheeks. "Haven't I already seen it?" she bantered back.

"You haven't seen anything yet, *wife*."

The sun was starting to dip low in the sky when they reined their horses in before entering the mountain pass. Shadows lined the trail as Porter shifted the reins to his left hand and pulled out his revolver.

He gave Darcy a pointed look before he urged his horse forward. She understood his unspoken command; 'Be on your guard'.

Darcy followed his lead and pulled her derringer out of the pocket in her dress. After they arrived at the valley, Porter put up his hand as he halted his horse. His alert eyes scanned the wide valley, but his eyes narrowed at the far tip near the cave.

He pointed his revolver towards the cluster of trees that lined the mountain wall. Darcy tried to see what he was pointing at when something moved in the trees. It was the back end of a horse.

Porter dismounted, and she did the same. They hid their horses behind a large bush and cautiously approached the location where the horse was stashed. Porter stopped and put his fist up. He turned back towards her and whispered, "Stay here."

Before she could even respond, Porter crouched down low and ran towards where the lone horse was hidden. Darcy watched as he looked through the saddlebag and as his hand traced along the saddle. He seemed satisfied, because he quickly ran back over. "It is a horse from McCoy's ranch, but that saddle is recycled through the cowhands. I had hoped it was engraved with our suspect's initials."

"That would have been too convenient," she teased.

He gave her a disapproving look. "Agents do not make jokes while tracking a suspect."

"I must have missed that in basic training." To irk him even more, she smiled widely.

He sighed despairingly. "You are going to be the death of me, Mrs. Shaw."

My, that had a nice ring to it, she thought.

"It is too much of a coincidence that someone from McCoy's cattle ranch is up here at this hour," Porter said in a hushed voice. "We must assume that this is our suspect and proceed with caution." He stepped closer to her and brought his hand up to trail his knuckles along her right cheekbone. "Please be careful."

"I'm ready," she replied earnestly.

"I am serious," he insisted. "If shooting starts, I want you to stay hidden." She opened her mouth to protest when he placed his calloused finger over her lips. "I won't be able to be an effective agent if I am worried about you."

Darcy met his gaze and saw his face was full of worry. For her. She didn't want to discount his feelings, but she needed to stand up for herself. She was a Lady Pinkerton. She brought up her hand and lowered his finger from her lips. "You need to learn to trust me as your partner."

He leaned closer until his forehead was touching hers. "I do trust you, but I can't lose you."

"I'm not going anywhere," she murmured.

Porter swallowed slowly, as if he was trying to bury his emotions. "Follow me," he ordered in a hoarse voice. He spun around and kept himself low to the ground as they walked up the path towards the cave. Stopping short, he said, "You will have to lead, because I don't know where the cave is."

She moved in front of him and started walking up the rocky terrain. Once they arrived at the cave, they pushed aside the bushes and saw the boulder had been rolled to the side, revealing the dark entrance. They lit their lanterns, drew their weapons, and crept further into the narrow cave until they could hear the distinctive clang of metal hitting rock.

Darcy held up the lantern towards the wall and saw water trickling down the rocks. The hint of gold flecks reflected off the light. She placed her derringer in her pocket and ran her fingers along the cold stone. They'd found the motive. Gold. And from the looks of it, this cave was full of it.

"Porter," she whispered. "Look at all this gold."

Porter held up his lantern and let out a low whistle. "You found a gold mine."

The sound of someone repeatedly hitting the stone surface continued to echo throughout the cave.

"Let's go see who is making all that racket, shall we?"

As they moved closer to the noise, the cave opened to reveal a stream running down the middle and rock formations hanging from the ceiling.

"This is beautiful and..." Her words stilled when a putrid smell assaulted her senses. She placed her hand in front of her nose to ward off the smell. "Do you smell that?"

"I do," Porter confirmed, moving his lantern in different directions. "It smells like death."

"That is what I was thinking."

They both spread out, attempting to find the source of that horrific smell. As Darcy turned the corner, she tripped over something. She turned her lantern towards the ground and saw a leg sticking out from an alcove. "Porter," she said in a hushed voice.

Porter walked towards her with an expectant look on his face. "Did you find something?" She pointed towards the boot, and he nodded. "Stay here," he ordered.

He headed back towards the alcove and she intentionally diverted her gaze. Decaying bodies were not something she wanted to see.

"I counted four dead bodies," Porter informed her, "and

they are in all stages of decomposition."

"Those poor men," she murmured.

Porter gave her an understanding look. "Don't worry. We'll get justice for those men and their families." He held his lantern up towards the repetitious noise of metal hitting rock. "We have dallied long enough. Let's go catch ourselves a murderer."

They moved until they saw a dimly lit area and the back of a man wielding a pickax. A candle was jammed into the wall, but it did not provide enough light to identify him. The man straightened and stretched his back. From this new angle, she could see that he was wearing a cap low on his head, a red handkerchief over his nose, and his clothes were so filthy that she had no idea what the color they were supposed to be.

Porter placed his hand back to corral her behind him. When she didn't comply immediately, he shot her a warning look. She realized that this was not the place to be disobeying his orders, so she stepped behind him. Unfortunately, she didn't move as quietly as she intended, and her boot slid against the gravel on the ground.

In a quick motion, the suspect tossed the pickax in their direction and it came barreling towards them. Porter shoved her out of the way before he jumped to the side. The suspect immediately blew out his candle and ran deeper into the cave. To her surprise, Porter extinguished his candle then rushed over to do the same to hers. Now they were all cloaked in darkness.

"The light makes us sitting ducks," he whispered as his left hand grabbed her hand. "Whatever happens, do not let go of my hand."

They pressed themselves up against the wall, waiting for the suspect to pass by them, but they felt no indication that he had done so. After waiting for what seemed like hours, Porter lit his lantern and started leading her back towards the entrance of the cave.

Unfortunately, they discovered the boulder had been shoved in front of the opening, allowing only a tiny finger of light to filter in. "Once we push this boulder out of the way, be prepared to shoot our way out of here," he warned.

They both pushed the boulder to the side but were met with only the sounds of nature. An owl hooted, and frogs croaked in the distance.

Porter kept low and charged out of the cave. He ran towards the cover of an outcropping of rocks about twenty yards away. He kept his pistol aimed in front of him, and his eyes roamed the mountain side. He let out a frustrated sigh. "The horse is gone," he shouted over at her.

Darcy looked back into the cave. "The suspect must have fled out of another entrance."

A hardened look came to Porter's eyes, one that she had not seen before. "We have narrowed down the suspect pool. It should be easy to figure out which cowhands were not in the bunkhouse tonight."

"Should we head back?"

"Not for a while," he replied. "We don't know if anyone is laying in wait for us past the mountain pass."

That seemed logical. "What should we do while we wait?"

Porter pulled out a deck of cards from his vest pocket. "We play cards."

An Agent for Darcy

Chapter 10

Porter was frying bacon when a yawning Darcy walked into the kitchen, wearing her white nightgown. He grabbed a cup, poured some milk into it and handed it to her. "You look exhausted," he said as he held out a chair for her.

"Good morning to you, as well," she replied, her tone grouchy.

Porter placed his left hand on the table and his right hand on the back of her chair. He leaned in and kissed her cheek. "Apparently, my wife becomes grumpy with lack of sleep."

Darcy took a sip of her milk before saying, "And my husband is unusually cheerful for someone who only got three hours of sleep last night."

"Pinkerton agents never sleep. That's our motto," he reminded her with a wink.

She yawned again. "I'm not a fan."

He chuckled as he straightened and walked back over to the

pan. "Regardless, you have signed up for this exciting life."

"Exciting?" she repeated. "Did I miss something?"

After flipping the bacon, he turned back towards her. "We played cards for hours," he pointed out.

"True," she replied with a half-smile, "it was fun beating you so soundly."

He grinned. "I recalled last night much differently."

There was a knock at the door and Darcy jumped up, sliding her hand into the pocket of her nightgown. She walked over to the door and asked, "Who is it?"

"Adam," came the muffled reply.

Darcy removed her hand from her pocket then opened the door. "Good morning, Mr. McCoy."

"I believe I have asked you to call me Adam on multiple occasions," he reminded her as he walked into the kitchen. "You both are a sight for sore eyes."

"Why is that?" Darcy asked as she sat back down at the table.

Adam tugged on his brown vest. "Last night before I went to bed, I came to check on you, but you weren't home. I ended up tossing and turning all night."

"Sorry about that. We were forced to hole up in the cave for a few hours until we were sure the coast was clear." Porter transferred the bacon onto a plate and placed it in the center of the table. "Eat up. I am making pancakes next. Trust me, you will need your strength for what we are about to tell you.

Lifting his brow, Adam asked Darcy, "Is he always this cheerful in the morning?"

"Apparently, so," she confirmed. "I need some time to adjust, but he is like a ray of sunshine."

"I wonder if we could bottle his enthusiasm and pass it along to the other cowhands," Adam jested.

Porter started mixing the pancake ingredients, ignoring their fun at his expense. "I am glad that you stopped by. When we searched the cave, we found the suspect inside, and he was mining for gold."

Adam groaned. "Ever since gold was found in Pike's Peak, everyone has had gold fever. Almost every stream gets panned, and every cave gets scrutinized."

Porter poured pancake batter into the sizzling pan. "This cave *is* a gold mine. Literally. It was filled with gold flecks."

Shooting up in his seat, Adam's eyes grew wide. "Seriously?"

Darcy nodded. "The gold reflected off the lantern."

"I'll be darned," Adam replied thoughtfully. "So, someone was willing to kill to keep us out of the valley."

As he flipped the pancakes, Porter revealed, "The suspect rode in on a horse from your ranch, but we were unable to identify him. Which cowhands weren't in the bunkhouse last night?"

Adam's voice grew hard as he said, "So it was one of my men that betrayed us all."

"It was," Darcy responded with sympathy in her voice. "We assumed that was the case since your wife was murdered in your house, but we had no proof."

Shoving back his chair, Adam stood up and placed his hands on the back of his head. "When I get my hands on whoever did this…" he paused, and dropped his hands, "I'm going to kill them."

Porter removed the pancakes from the pan. "No, you are going to let us do our job and arrest whoever is responsible for the murder of your wife and cowhands." He placed the plate onto the table. "We need you to focus, not go off half-cocked. Which cowhands weren't in the bunkhouse last night?"

Adam sat back down in his chair and placed his forearms on the table. "Every other night the men rotate who sleeps with the cattle. Last night, it was the crew that played cards with Darcy the night before."

Porter tensed at that admission. His wife had been sitting near a cold-blooded killer, and she had no idea. Darcy must have felt his tension, because she placed her hand on his sleeve reassuringly.

"Of those men, who do you think would resort to killing to keep that mine a secret?" Darcy asked.

Adam winced. "I have known most of these men all of my life. Their fathers were cowhands for my dad and so on. I can't imagine any of them being so ruthless. Besides, they all loved Amanda."

Porter took his fork and jabbed it into the pile of pancakes. "Be that as it may be, one or more of these men are killers. Any leads that you could give us would be well appreciated."

"Again, I vouch for my brother, Ralph..." Adam's voice trailed off as Darcy and Porter exchanged a look. "What?

Porter gave him a stern look. "Ralph is our main suspect."

"That's ridiculous!" Adam exclaimed.

Darcy looked him in the eye. "Ralph has a temper, and I saw him fight with you in your kitchen. Furthermore, he was pressing for a fence to be built to block off the valley."

"Of course he was," Adam stated. "He is tired of the other cowhands turning up missing. We all are."

"We saw their bodies in the cave," Porter informed him with a solemn expression.

Adam wiped a hand over his face as he sat in stunned silence. "I had assumed they were dead, but a part of me was still holding out hope."

"I am sorry for your losses," Darcy murmured.

"If you don't think Ralph could be behind this, then who do *you* suspect?" Porter asked, refocusing the conversation.

Adam placed his elbow on the table and dropped his face into his hand. "Don is the cook and rarely comes out of the bunkhouse. When he does, it is only to complain about something. Bill and Butch are hard-working cowhands, but they never went to school. They were working beside their old man from the time they could walk."

"Murderers don't need to be educated," Porter said before he took a bite of his pancakes.

"True, but I would be hard pressed to believe it was them," Adam asserted. "Perry comes off as gruff and unapproachable, but he has a tender heart. He just replied to an advertisement for a mail order bride. I find it difficult that he would resort to murder while he is waiting for a bride."

Darcy reached for a slice of bacon and brought it up to her mouth. After taking a bite, she replied, "This is delicious, Porter."

Porter gave her an impish smile. "I am a man of many talents. Perhaps I could show you some more later," he asked, his eyes darting towards her lips.

Darcy's eyes grew wide as she turned her attention back

towards the table. He loved teasing his bride. She was such an innocent in so many ways.

Adam's voice broke through his thoughts. "Tom is young and gets excited about the most mundane things."

"Which leaves us with Dustin and John?" Darcy prodded.

"It couldn't be either one of them," Adam said with a shake of his head. "Dustin and John worked for Amanda's father before we got married."

Porter rose and picked up his plate. "Did any of these men ever have a problem with your wife?"

"John tried to court Amanda the same time I came around," Adam revealed, "but she never showed him any real attention."

Darcy pressed her lips together before asking, "Did John ever show Amanda any type of favor after you two were married?"

"I know what you are thinking, and it's not possible," Adam insisted.

After cleaning his dish, Porter said, "Whether you like it or not, there is a murderer on your ranch."

Adam stood and shoved in his chair. "I just can't believe it could be any one of my men. If you will excuse me."

Porter and Darcy watched as Adam walked out of the cottage, closing the door behind him.

Darcy spoke first. "I played cards with those men. I didn't suspect any of them had nefarious intentions."

Porter came to sit down next to her. "Criminals allow you to see what they want you to see. They are smooth talkers and generally come across as likeable people. However, in my experience, they switch between two extremes."

Darcy bit her lower lip as she appeared to concentrate on his words. "What is the next step?"

"We lure him out."

Furrowing her brows, she asked, "How do we do that?"

Porter reached out and placed his hand over hers. "Do you trust me?" he asked intently.

Her eyes held tenderness. "Wholeheartedly."

"Then, it's time to inform the cowhands that we found gold in the valley."

"Is that wise?"

Porter gave her a lopsided grin. "If my plan works, then the murderer will target me."

"And if he doesn't?"

"My plans always work," he joked.

She laughed. "It must be hard to have an ego as large as yours."

"It is a cross that I must bear."

"I should go change for the day," she said, rising.

Not releasing her hand, he replied, "I was pleased to see you took my advice about carrying your gun everywhere you go."

She leaned closer with a playful gleam in her eyes. "You will learn, husband, that I do, on occasion, take your advice."

To his complete astonishment, she kissed him on the cheek. A tender, loving kiss that seemed to linger. Or was that just his wishful thinking? She stepped back and diverted her gaze before she rushed out of the room.

Porter spun around in his seat and watched her race out. After a long moment, he realized that he was still smiling.

Porter dismounted and led his horse to the watering trough. He had spent the morning moving the cattle, and he was grateful for the break in the saddle. Even though he loved the thrill of being a Pinkerton agent, he certainly enjoyed the life of a cowboy. This life was as familiar to him as breathing.

Earlier this morning, he had let it slip to John and Perry about discovering gold in the valley, and now he was waiting to see if the murderer would slip up.

Tom ran up to him with an excited look on his face. "Is it true?"

"What?" he asked, careful to play his role convincingly.

"Did you find gold in the valley?"

Porter stepped closer and lowered his voice. "I did. There is gold everywhere in those caves."

Tom's eyes gleamed with interest. "Do you have any?"

"It is not mine to take," he replied. "It is on Adam's property. His gold."

"You didn't even take a little nugget?" Tom asked, glancing over his shoulder. "It would be our secret."

"Nah, I prefer to keep my job," Porter stated matter-of-factly.

"Bailey!" Ralph shouted in a gruff tone near the barn. "I need to speak with you." Without waiting for a response, he walked into the barn.

Tom let out an amused howl. "You are in for it now."

"What did I do?" he asked, pretending to look nervous.

"Who knows with Ralph," Tom said with a shrug. "But his bark is worse than his bite."

"Well, I better get this over with," he muttered under his breath. As he neared the barn, he placed his hand in the back of his trousers to confirm that his revolver was still concealed underneath his vest.

"Ralph?" he asked, walking further into the room.

Suddenly, he was shoved back against the wall and Ralph's forearm was against his throat. Ralph leaned closer to him, his lips snarled. "You need to stop spreading this nonsense," he growled.

"What nonsense is that?" Porter had no doubt that he was stronger than Ralph, but he needed to let Ralph believe he was in charge.

Ralph shoved his forearm further into his throat, causing him to take shallow breaths. "The gold. There is no gold up in those caves, and you are cruel to even give these men false hope." He loosened his forearm. "Your spouting nonsense ends now. Do I make myself clear?"

Porter had looked into the eyes of cold-blooded killers before and lived to tell about it. But Ralph's eyes held no evil glint, but more determination. He even detected a hint of sadness in his words. Porter knew in that instant that Ralph was not their man.

Taking control of the situation, Porter shoved Ralph back and the force caused him to tumble to the ground. Ralph's eyes narrowed as he stared up at him, and he looked as if he was ready to brawl.

"Stand down," Porter ordered. "It is my turn to ask the questions."

"You are in no position to question me," Ralph scoffed as he rose.

Porter took a commanding step towards him. "I am here on your brother's request."

"Of course you are," Ralph declared. "Adam hired you because we had cowhands go missing."

"They aren't missing. They are dead," he confirmed.

Ralph wiped his hands on his trousers. "That doesn't surprise me, but where's your proof?"

"I saw them," he revealed.

"You saw them? Where?" Ralph asked suspiciously.

Porter had never been led astray when he trusted his instinct, but that didn't mean he didn't verify facts before giving away his advantage. "Why do you hate your brother so much?"

Ralph lifted his brow at his question. "Who told you that I hate my brother?"

"My wife saw you fighting in the kitchen."

"We fight all the time," he said. "We're brothers."

"Step-brothers," Porter corrected.

Ralph glared at him. "Who told you that?"

Seeing no reason to deny it, he responded, "Adam. He told me the whole story of how you arrived at the ranch and how you were cut out of the will."

Ralph turned and walked towards the stalls where the horses were kept. "Why would Adam tell you that?"

Rather than answer his question, he pressed, "Do you resent Adam?"

Ralph spun around. "No. I have no ill feelings towards my brother. Besides, he was kind enough to give me a hundred cattle for my own brand."

"Why are you so against me revealing that there is gold in the valley?" he asked, stepping closer.

Sighing, Ralph leaned back against a stall. "If Adam told you the whole story then you would know."

"He left that part out."

Ralph kicked at the straw on the ground before sharing, "From my earliest memories, my mother was obsessed with finding gold. We were out in streams panning all day, every day. The day my mother died was the first day I could recall not going down to the stream."

"Did she ever find any gold?"

Ralph winced. "Only a few flakes here and there."

"How did you survive?" Porter asked, his tone softening.

"My mom was a saloon girl," Ralph confessed. "Every morning and afternoon, we were at the streams, and at night, I was left alone while she went to work." He looked up with an intensity in his eyes. "Coming to live with my father and Adam was the best thing that ever happened to me."

Porter nodded. "I believe you."

Chuckling, Ralph replied dryly, "Well, I'm sure glad for that." He grew serious. "Sorry about the interrogation earlier. Gold makes people go crazy, and I didn't want that frenzy to come to the ranch. We already have someone targeting cowboys."

Reaching into his pocket, Porter removed his Pinkerton badge and held it up. "I was hired by your brother to investigate the deaths of the four cowhands."

To his astonishment, a wide smile broke out on Ralph's face, making him appear much younger than his twenty-one years. "You're a *real* Pinkerton agent. I can't believe it. I have heard so many stories about the bravery of the men at your agency."

"I need you to focus," Porter said, unfamiliar with such a positive reaction, "because I need your help."

"Anything," Ralph replied, but his smile didn't dim.

"We have narrowed down the suspect list to only a handful of the cowhands."

"Which are?"

"The men that weren't in the bunkhouse last night," Porter

stated, keeping his gaze firmly on Ralph. "Have any of those men been acting suspicious lately?"

"No. You got it wrong," Ralph asserted. "None of those men would turn on each other. We cowhands have to stick together."

Porter decided to try a different tactic. "The night that Amanda was killed, I understand you stayed behind to brand some calves."

"That's correct," Ralph answered slowly.

"Who was with you?"

Ralph tilted his head for a moment before saying, "Dustin and John. They could vouch for me."

"Vouch? I am not looking for them to vouch for you," he said. "I believe Dustin or John could be the killer."

Ralph started shaking his head profusely. "Not possible."

"Let me ask you another question. When the cowhands went missing, where were Dustin and John?"

There was a long pause before Ralph replied hesitantly, "Sleeping near the cattle."

Porter stepped closer. "Between those two men, did either of them have a problem with Amanda?"

"Adam's wife?" Ralph asked in confusion. "No one had trouble with Amanda. She was beloved among the cowhands."

His face paled when realization dawned on what he was asking. "You think someone killed her?" he asked in a hushed voice. "*Impossible.*"

"Not impossible," he confirmed, "very plausible."

"Well, neither John or Dustin could be responsible. Both knew Amanda before she married Adam. John even tried to court her."

Porter knew he wasn't asking the right question. Ralph knew more than he realized, but he needed to draw that information out. Trying again, he asked, "On the night that Amanda died, did either Dustin or John visit the house. For any reason?"

"All of us did," Ralph admitted. "Amanda made us supper early that night. She was alive when we left."

"We know that Amanda drank a cup of tea that night. Do you know when?"

"Right after dinner, because I remember John heated the water for her."

Finally! A lead. "Thank you, Ralph. You have been very helpful," he declared as he ran towards the door. Before he exited the barn, he spun back around. "I need you to keep our conversation private, at least until after we close this case."

Ralph wore a baffled look. "I can do that, but I'm afraid I didn't share anything that was useful to you."

"You're wrong," Porter proclaimed before he exited the barn.

An Agent for Darcy

Chapter 11

Darcy had just finished cleaning the table in Adam's house when the door opened, and John slipped through.

"Morning, John," she greeted cheerfully.

John's usual charming demeanor was stripped away, and his eyes held anger. "You need to tell your husband to stop yapping about the gold in the valley."

"I beg your pardon?" Her hand slid into the pocket of her dress until she gripped her derringer, providing her with immediate reassurance.

He advanced towards her, stopping only a few feet from her. "Gold makes men do crazy things."

She tilted her head up to meet his gaze and replied, "I am not sure what this has to do with me."

John's lips curled downward at her defiant response. He took a step closer. "You tell Porter that he better stop talking about the gold or else."

"Or else what?"

His eyes narrowed. "Just relay the message."

"No," she insisted. "I am not a messenger. If you want to give Porter a message, then do it yourself."

John took another step closer so there was no space between them. "Listen, Mrs. Bailey," he drawled, "you have no idea the danger that Porter has put you both in."

"Perhaps you could explain it to me."

His expression grew hard. "You have been warned," he said, his words menacing.

"If you are going to threaten me, at least tell me why." She wanted to draw out this conversation and hopefully gain some information in the process.

He laughed coldly. "I am not the one that you need to fear."

"What does that mean?" she asked, rearing back.

"Be on your guard, Mrs. Bailey. Someone is killing to ensure secrets stay buried."

John spun around and left without saying another word, leaving Darcy speechless. If she didn't need to fear John, then who did she need to protect herself from? She needed more answers. She ran towards the door to chase after him, but it opened right in front of her.

A stern-faced Dustin stood in the doorway, blocking her

from exiting. "I just came to check on you, ma'am. I saw John storm out of here, and I wanted to make sure everything was all right."

"I actually was going to catch up with him and finish our conversation," she answered.

Dustin glanced over his shoulder, not moving an inch from his position. "John seems to be in a foul mood. I would give him some time to cool off."

"I suppose so," Darcy murmured as she took a few steps back.

His expression softened as he asked, "Is there something amiss? Something that I can help you with?"

She offered him a forced smile. "You are too kind, but John and I were having a disagreement."

"John is not one to be quick to anger," Dustin commented. "I wonder why he was angry with you."

Not willing to discuss her previous conversation with him, Darcy inquired, "Is there something I can help you with?"

Dustin shook his head. "No, ma'am." He tipped his hat at her. "I hope you have a good day."

Darcy watched as Dustin closed the door behind him. Both conversations seemed strange, and it left her with an uneasy feeling. She sighed at her thoughts. She was a Pinkerton agent. She would not be coerced or frightened. After all, she knew that

Porter's plan would involve risks to lure out the murderer, and she was prepared.

Her mind barely registered the sound of boots approaching her from behind before everything went black.

Porter jogged up the few steps of Adam's house and opened the kitchen door. When he didn't see Darcy in the kitchen, he shouted, "Darcy!"

He stopped and waited for her response. When none was forthcoming, he started searching the house for her. Where was she? Did she go back to their cottage?

He had a bad feeling in the pit of his stomach as he stormed out of the kitchen and raced to their cottage. When he slammed opened the door, he found no evidence of Darcy. He stepped out onto their porch and yelled, "Darcy!"

This morning, they had held hands as he walked her to Adam's house before he started his shift. They had parted on good terms, so he knew she wouldn't have left on her own accord. Which meant someone had taken her. But who?

John came to his mind. Porter sprinted down the steps, and his eyes scanned the surrounding buildings and corrals. He was not a man to be trifled with under most circumstances, and someone was foolish enough to have snatched his wife right from under him. Only this person did not know what great lengths he was willing to go to get Darcy back.

In a short period of time, Darcy had become the most important thing in his world, and he had no intention of letting her go. He planned to confess his feelings to Darcy as soon as this case was over and truly make her his wife.

Porter's eyes landed on John as he walked near the bunkhouse. Storming across the yard, he didn't stop until he shoved John against the side of the bunkhouse. He pulled out his revolver and placed it under John's chin.

"Where is my wife?" he growled.

"How would I know?" John defended, his voice shaking with fear. "When I left her at the house, she was perfectly fine."

He cocked his pistol. "Wrong answer. My wife is missing. You have five seconds to tell me where she is."

"I don't know!" John exclaimed. "I tried to warn her."

"Warn her about what?" he asked, pressing the barrel deeper into John's skin.

"Porter! What do you think you are doing?" Adam shouted as he ran closer to them. "Put down your weapon."

"No," Porter contended. "This is the man that killed your wife!"

Adam's eyes lit up with rage as he charged between them,

pushing Porter out of the way. Swinging back his fist, Adam punched John in the stomach and then his jaw.

John fell back against the bunkhouse and put his hands up in front of him to protect himself. "You have it all wrong. I didn't kill Amanda. I loved her!"

"She was my wife," Adam stated. "Or did you forget that?"

"No, I did not forget that," John replied, annoyance in his tone. "She chose you because you had a nice spread, and I was only a cowhand."

"Amanda loved me," Adam said firmly.

John shook his head. "No, she did not. She loved me!"

Porter grabbed a fist full of John's shirt and yanked him towards him. "If you loved her so much, then why did you kill her?"

"I didn't kill her," John defended. "Are you not listening to anything that I said?"

"You don't seem surprised by the fact that Amanda was murdered," Porter pointed out.

John's eyes grew pensive. "She wasn't supposed to die."

Loosening his grip on John's shirt, he ordered, "Explain."

"No, I'm not saying nothing," John spat out.

Porter shoved John back against the bunkhouse. "Let's string him up. He admitted to knowing about Amanda's death."

"I'll get the rope," Adam agreed.

But before he took his first step, John shouted, "No! Wait! Let me explain."

"You have one minute." Adam crossed his arms over his chest.

"Dustin had acquired some arsenic because of the rats in the barn," John attempted to say. "Somehow it must have gotten into Amanda's tea and…"

Adam grunted in disgust. "We are wasting our time. I'm getting the rope."

"Wait!" John took a step towards Adam, and Porter slammed him against the bunkhouse.

Porter put his forearm to John's throat. "It's illegal to purchase arsenic. So save us your lies and tell us the truth before I lose my patience."

John's eyes grew fearful. "Somehow Dustin obtained the arsenic, and he wanted to kill Mr. McCoy." He shifted his gaze towards Adam. "But Amanda refused to kill you, and Dustin accused her of betraying him."

"Amanda betraying Dustin?" Adam questioned. "You aren't making any sense."

Surprised by this turn of events, Porter removed his forearm from John's throat. "Start from the beginning."

John tenderly rubbed his neck before saying, "Over two months ago, Amanda found a cave in the valley, a cave that was filled with gold. She rushed to tell Dustin and me."

"Even if that was true," Adam probed, "why did she tell you and Dustin about this cave? Why not me?"

"Amanda begged you to leave the ranch and travel to see the world," John explained, "but you refused. You refused all her requests to leave this god-forsaken town."

"Of course, I refused. I had a ranch to run!" Adam shouted, tossing his arms up in the air.

"Amanda hated it here and was aching to leave," John huffed.

Adam's hands balled up into fists as he explained, "Once she was with child, she would have settled down and been content."

"Amanda married you because you were the richest man in the territory. She wanted adventure, and you locked her up in a ranch in the middle of nowhere," John stated in disgust. "You stifled her, and she resented you for it."

Porter frowned as he saw the crestfallen look on Adam's face and realized that John had spoken the truth. "If you had the gold mine, then why did you start killing the cowhands? Why not just mine the gold?"

"Dustin killed them," John stated. "He got gold fever

something fierce and spent all of his free time at the mine."

"You are trying to blame Dustin for everything," Adam accused.

"No, it's true," John contended. "Six weeks ago, Trevor caught Dustin in the valley with a lantern and a chisel. He killed him. That is when he hatched the plan to force you away from the valley." He glared at Adam. "Unfortunately, you refused to take the warning, and Dustin had to kill more people to keep our secret."

Adam clenched his jaw so tightly that a muscle pulsated under his ear. "And Amanda went along with all of this."

John looked forlorn. "No. She was against it and even threatened to tell the sheriff if Dustin didn't stop killing."

Porter lifted his brow. "How did Dustin respond to that threat?"

"I had no idea that he planned to kill her. I swear it!" John defended himself. "Amanda was kind enough to make us dinner the night she died, and I even boiled the water for her tea. Dustin put the arsenic in the sugar container and brought it to her. Amanda kept dumping more and more into her tea, saying it wasn't sweet enough. Dustin kept her distracted by talking, so she didn't realize it wasn't really sugar."

Porter closed his eyes. "If it was arsenic, then she wouldn't have detected any change in flavor."

"Exactly," John replied. "The next day, I went in to say good morning, and I found her sprawled out on the ground."

"And you just left her?" Adam grunted.

"I had no choice. I confronted Dustin about it, and he denied it at first," John said. "However, he threatened to reveal Amanda's and my close relationship if I even breathed a word of my suspicions. He said he wouldn't rest until he dragged her name into the mud like the whore that she was."

"How close were you two, exactly?" Adam asked, his tone taking on a hard edge.

"Very…" John started to say as Adam punched him in the jaw, knocking him to the ground.

"You are going to hang for your crimes!" Adam exclaimed, standing over him.

John rubbed his reddened jaw. "I didn't kill nobody. It was all Dustin."

Tucking his pistol into his gun belt, Porter narrowed his eyes at John. "Dustin abducted Darcy, and you are going to help us stop him."

John looked between them with disbelief on his features. "No. Absolutely not. Dustin has killed four highly capable cowboys. What makes you any different?"

"I am a Pinkerton agent, as is Darcy," Porter informed him. "And if you help us, I will put in a good word to the sheriff. It could save you from the noose."

"I knew there was something different about your wife," John stated with approval in his tone. "Fine. I will help you, but only because I owe it to Amanda to stop her killer. Not because of him." He jerked his thumb towards Adam.

Adam's glare intensified. "I don't trust him. He will betray us at his first opportunity."

Porter placed his hand over his pistol. "If I even suspect that John is betraying us, I will kill him where he stands." He turned his gaze towards the wide expansive green fields. "Where do you think Dustin would take Darcy?"

"The cave," John confirmed, "and I know where the back entrance is."

An Agent for Darcy

Chapter 12

Darcy awoke to the sound of metal hitting rock. She opened her eyes, fighting back the desire to fall back into peaceful oblivion. The damp smell and the cold stone under her head told her that she was back in the cave.

Bringing her eyes up, she saw a candle jammed into the wall as Dustin repetitively hit the rock with his pickaxe. When a large chunk of rock fell to the ground, he laid his tool against the wall and picked it up.

She stifled a groan. Dustin was the murderer. How had they overlooked him? They'd been so focused on Ralph that he had escaped their notice.

His eyes admired the rock before he turned his gaze towards her. "You're finally awake."

She didn't feel the need to reply to his obvious statement, so she stayed quiet.

Dustin crouched down in front of her. "You and your husband have caused quite a stir with your rumors about finding gold in the valley." He held out the rock for her inspection. "Now, I will have to kill more people to keep this secret. Their deaths will be on your hands."

Darcy looked up at him in disbelief. "No. Their deaths are on *your* hands. You killed them."

He shrugged. "They were in the wrong place."

Sliding her hand into the right pocket of her dress, she realized her derringer was gone. Dustin laughed cruelly as he dropped the rock on the ground. "You actually thought I would let you keep your gun." He tsked. "You foolish, naive woman."

Straightening her back against the cold stone, she asked, "Why did you abduct me? Why not kill me like you did Amanda?"

To her surprise, Dustin slapped her right cheek, causing her head to hit the rock behind her. "What do you know about Amanda's death?"

"I know you killed her with arsenic," she replied, ignoring the ringing in her ears. "I found proof of it in her tea."

He grabbed her chin and yanked it down. "You are more than you appear, Mrs. Bailey. Lucky for me, I suspected you were much too knowledgeable to be a housekeeper." His gaze intensified. "So, who are you exactly?"

When she didn't answer, he slapped her again on her left cheek. "I can do this all day. Can you?"

Darcy's left hand grabbed the rock that Dustin had dropped. When he brought up his hand to strike her again, she slammed it hard against his head.

Dustin roared in pain as he fell to the ground. Darcy jumped up and tried to run further into the cave, despite it being pitch black all around her. She tripped and nearly fell, catching herself on a rock outcropping. Realizing that Dustin would surely catch her if she fell again, she rushed along as fast as she dared through the darkness, stumbling over the rough ground, feeling her way along the walls.

"Darcy!" Dustin screamed from behind her. "There is no place for you to go. When I find you, I will take pleasure in beating you before I kill you."

Daring to glance over her shoulder, she saw Dustin held the candle high in the air as he slowly trailed after her. If she attempted to hide, he could still find her with the light. No, she had to keep moving.

Her boot clipped a stone, and she stumbled forward, sliding and skidding along on her hands. Tears burned her eyes from the pain as she jumped up and tried to move faster. Her breath came in ragged gasps, but she didn't dare stop. She knew what her fate would be if he caught her.

Someone grabbed her upper arm, yanked her to the side, and covered her mouth. She tried to scream but the hand muffled the noise. "Darcy, it's me," Porter whispered next to her ear.

She whimpered in relief and turned in his arms, wrapping her arms around his waist. He pressed her tightly against him. "I have you now. You're safe."

"I know," Darcy whispered.

From the moment she had met Porter Shaw, she had felt safe and protected, not only in his arms, but in his presence as well. And she had no doubt in her heart, that he was a good, kind man, and it was not just for show.

Porter kissed the top of her head. "John will escort you to safety. I will deal with Dustin."

"I believe I also asked to help." That was Adam's voice next to her.

"Fine," Porter acknowledged, "but you do not get a discount on our payment if you get shot."

Adam chuckled. "Fair enough."

"Darcy!" Dustin shouted, his voice echoing off the rocks. "I know you're in here."

"John," Porter stated in a hushed voice. "Take Darcy out the back and don't stop until she is out of harm's way."

She tightened her grip around Porter's waist. "I don't want to leave you."

Porter placed his hands behind his back and forced her hands away from his waist. "Please, Darcy. I need you to be safe. Your life is more important than mine."

"You are wrong about that, but I will go because you asked nicely," she said, knowing they didn't have the luxury of time to argue.

"Finally, you see reason," he teased, pressing a pistol into her hand. "Here is my spare gun. Now run to safety, and you have my permission to shoot John for *any* infraction."

John lit a candle and reached for her hand. "Let's go before Dustin catches us."

As they stepped onto the path, a shot rang out, causing John to crumble to the floor. Immediately, the candle flamed out, cloaking them once again in darkness. Darcy scurried back towards the wall where she left Porter, and he placed his left arm protectively around her waist.

"New plan," Porter declared. "We stop Dustin from killing us."

"I'm amenable to that plan," Adam jested nervously.

"Who did I just shoot?" Dustin's mocking voice grew closer. "If I'm lucky, it was Porter."

All three of them cocked their pistols and waited until Dustin came into view.

To their surprise, Adam stepped out from behind the safety of the rock and proclaimed, "Dustin. I know what you did, and I know why."

"Adam?" Dustin asked in surprise. The illumination of his candle allowed them to see him approaching them. "What are you doing here?"

Adam held up his revolver towards Dustin. "I can't let you hurt anyone else."

"Well, this will save me the trouble of killing you later," Dustin declared, seeming unphased by the pistol pointed at him.

"Why Amanda?" Adam asked. "Why did you have to kill my wife?"

Dustin stopped a short distance away, holding his gun in his left hand. "I did you a favor. She and John were consorting on the side, and she was playing you for a fool."

"She didn't deserve to die," Adam said, his voice strained. "I loved her."

"She didn't love you. She loved your money, your power, but eventually she would have left you," Dustin revealed. "You were supposed to be her ticket out of this town, but instead you became her warden."

"I never forced Amanda to stay!" Adam shouted.

"Amanda was tired of being a rancher's wife. She wanted to leave you and start over. But in order to do that, she needed money… lots and lots of money."

"Why did you kill her?"

"Let's just say that she didn't approve of my methods," Dustin hedged. "Besides, I didn't want to share. This gold mine belongs to me."

"So, you killed four of your friends?" Adam asked in shock.

"They weren't my friends," Dustin replied without a shred of remorse. "Neither are you. Once I kill you, nothing will stop me from mining all this gold and living the good life for the rest of my days."

"I would have shared the gold with you," Adam stated.

Dustin let out a bark of laughter. "No, you wouldn't have. Besides, I already told you, I don't want to share with anyone." He brought up his pistol and fired it at Adam.

Adam ducked behind the rock and looked over at them. "What now?"

"A good, old-fashioned shootout," Porter said, before he pointed his pistol at Dustin and fired.

Dustin's candle dropped to the ground and everything went black except for the occasional spark of a gun as it was fired.

Crouching low, Porter grabbed Darcy's hand and whispered over to Adam, "We need to get out of here."

"If I recall correctly, if we stay close to this wall, it will take us back to the entrance," Adam replied.

Porter gripped Darcy's hand tighter as Dustin fired another round, hitting the rock they were hiding behind. "Stay low and try not to die." Holding Darcy's hand tightly, he started to move towards what he hoped was the entrance.

The darkness that surrounded them was oppressive as Porter kept his other hand on the cold, damp wall, hoping that they were going the right way. If not, they would be forced to light their lantern, and Dustin would be able to pick them off one-by-one.

Up ahead, Porter saw a sliver of light and breathed a sigh of relief. They had found the back entrance. None of them stopped running until they emerged into a grove of trees.

They had escaped from the cave, but there was still Dustin to contend with. But first, he needed to get Darcy to safety. "Run, Darcy!" Porter encouraged, letting go of her hand. "Further up the trail is John's horse. I will meet you back at the ranch."

"No," Darcy said, standing her ground. "I am a Pinkerton agent, just like you. Let me prove my worth."

Porter closed the distance between them and placed a hand on her cheek. "I already know what you are worth, and it is far greater than I will ever be." His eyes held an intensity that she did not understand. "It is not a matter of letting you prove that you are a good agent, because I already know that. It is a matter of you not getting hurt, because *I love you*."

Adam cleared his throat. "That was touching, but we have a mad man barreling after us. Do you think you could wrap this up anytime soon?"

"Run, Darcy," he pleaded.

Darcy placed her hand over his. "I go where you go. We are partners," she replied, her voice firm. "Besides, there are three of us and only one of him."

"Yeah, but that Dustin is a whole lot of crazy," Adam pointed out.

Porter didn't know if he wanted to strangle Darcy or kiss her, but now was not the time. He needed to trust her. "Fine. Everyone station yourself behind a tree and shoot to kill. Dustin has no qualms about killing all three of us."

Time seemed to slow as they waited for Dustin to emerge from the cave. Where was he? He should have been close behind them. What if he had circled back and exited into the valley?

A pistol cocked from behind Porter, and he felt the cold barrel of a pistol pressed against his head. "You didn't know there was a third entrance to the cave, did you?" Dustin mocked.

Porter heard another pistol cocking, only this time he heard his wife's voice. "I am going to have to insist that you lower your gun from my husband's head."

"Sure thing, little lady," Dustin said, removing the barrel from Porter's head.

Porter jumped out of the way and spun around to see Dustin elbowing Darcy in the face, knocking her to the ground and pointing his pistol at her.

"No!" Porter screamed. He ran and jumped in front of Darcy, just as the gun went off, hitting him in the chest.

Porter heard two revolvers discharge before everything went black.

Chapter 13

Darcy opened the door to the cottage as Adam carried an unconscious Porter over his shoulder. "Put him on the kitchen table," she ordered.

Adam hesitated, looking quite unsure about her command. "On the table?"

"Yes. It'll be easier to operate if I'm not doing it on my hands and knees," she explained, trying to keep the desperation out of her voice.

"Understood," Adam said as he followed her instructions and stepped back. "Now what?"

"I'm going to remove the bullet and stitch him up." She ran into her room, tossed open her trunk, and grabbed her medical bag. When she stepped back into the kitchen, she gave Adam a pointed look. "I need whiskey, *now!*"

Adam nodded and ran out of the cottage, closing the door behind him. Darcy walked up to Porter and tenderly stroked his right cheek. He loved her! She closed her eyes as a tear leaked out and ran down her cheek. "Please don't leave me," she pleaded.

Porter's moan snapped her back into the present. Taking a pair of scissors from her bag, she cut through his blood-soaked shirt. She pulled it back, revealing a bullet wound in his right shoulder. She noted the dark, red hole still oozing thick blood.

Darcy had tended multiple gunshot wound patients over the years, but she had never been the one to remove the bullet. She had always assisted the doctor with that procedure. Well, it was her time now.

As she washed her hands, Adam opened the door, with a glass bottle in his hand. "Generously pour the whiskey over the wound and prepare to hold him down," she directed over her shoulder.

Adam unscrewed the lid as he walked over to Porter and poured the whiskey over the bullet wound. Porter let out a loud wail of pain and started thrashing on the table. Adam placed his forearm on Porter's chest and shoved him back down.

Darcy gently placed her hand on Porter's left shoulder. "It'll be alright. You have to trust us."

At the sound of her voice, Porter began to relax against the table.

"Porter," she began, "this is going to hurt. I need to remove the bullet. Do you want something to bite down on?"

Porter shook his head and clutched the table with his right hand, clenching his jaw.

Taking her fingers, she pressed it into the oozing wound, ignoring her husband's sharp intake of breath. She kept digging around until she felt the unmistakable tip of the bullet. Squeezing her fingers around the metal, she pulled it out.

Grabbing the bottle of whiskey, she poured it over the wound to clean it out again. Porter cried out and started thrashing again.

Adam leaned harder on Porter's chest as Darcy reached for her needle.

"Dearest," she said, laying her hand on his cheek, "I am going to stitch you up."

Once again, her voice seemed to soothe him. Darcy poured alcohol over the needle, removed the catgut from her medical bag, and threaded it through. She stitched the bullet wound closed, then stepped back. Pleased that there was no seepage, she sighed. "We have done all that we can. Now, it's his turn."

Darcy tenderly wiped the sweat off Porter's brow with a cloth. She leaned down and kissed him on his forehead, her lips lingering. "You have to live, Porter. I can't live without you," she pleaded in a soft voice.

"I'll take him to the bed," Adam said, stepping closer to the table.

Darcy stepped back and noticed her blood-covered hands. "Thank you. I will see to this mess."

For the next while, she scrubbed the table and floor to a pristine clean. Her back ached, her muscles were sore, but she did not care. The image of Porter's limp body kept replaying in her mind. What was he thinking jumping in front of her? The sad thing was, she knew exactly what he was thinking. He was saving her life. A grief-filled sob escaped her lips at that thought. Curse him for being so selfless! She didn't want to live without him. She couldn't live without him, especially since she knew he loved her.

Adam's voice broke through her thoughts as she sat on the kitchen floor. "Darcy," he started, "are you all right?"

"Yes," she replied, not bothering to look up.

"Liar," he teased. "You're barely keeping it together."

She rose and wrapped her arms around her waist. Not wanting to talk about herself, she asked, "How are you doing?"

"Splendid," Adam replied, dropping onto the sofa. "I just found out that my whole life has been a lie. My wife never loved me, and she was consorting with one of my cowhands."

Darcy walked over and sat next to him. "My last husband was shot at a brothel when it was discovered he and his mistress were planning on killing me off."

Adam stared at her for a moment, then he chuckled wryly.

"I see you can relate."

"I can," she said. "I felt embarrassed, angry, grief-stricken, bitter, sad…" Her voice trailed off as she lowered her eyes. "I was furious that I hadn't seen any of the signs. I started blaming myself for all my husband's misdeeds, and I punished myself by hiding away."

Angling his body on the sofa, he faced her and asked, "How did you overcome all those obstacles?"

Darcy brought her gaze up. "I started to trust again, knowing that I couldn't do it alone." She reached out and encompassed his hand. "So many people have told me these words, but I wasn't ready to hear them. I hope you are, because it will save you much torment." She hesitated, hoping her eyes confirmed the truthfulness of her words. "You did nothing wrong. This was not your fault. Do not punish yourself for other's mistakes."

"Thank you." Tears came to Adam's eyes and slid down his cheeks. "How do I go on from here?"

She tightened her hold on his hand, feeling compelled to share part of her story. "Five days ago, I was assigned to this case on the condition that I married my trainer."

"Five days ago?" he asked in confusion. "But you must have known Porter prior to that?"

She shook her head. "No. I was hired, and we married

within moments of meeting each other."

"But…" Adam looked back towards the bedroom. "Why?"

"For propriety's sake, a Lady Pinkerton must marry an agent for her first case."

"What happens after that?"

"We have two options. We can get an annulment and start working separate cases," she explained, "or we could stay married and continue to work together."

Adam turned his hopeful gaze towards her. "What if you stayed with me?"

"Pardon?" she asked, withdrawing her hand from his.

"I find you fascinating, and I think we would suit," he began, "not now, of course. But in the future. I would never hurt you, and I would be faithful. For the mean time, you could stay on as my housekeeper… and think of the gold." He waved his hand in the air. "You could have anything your heart desired."

As she listened to his words, Darcy felt honored by his jumbled marriage proposal. He was not seeking a marriage of convenience, but he was offering her something much greater… his shattered heart. "Adam…"

He put his hand up, silencing her. "We both have similar backgrounds, and we understand each other. You can't leave me, because I don't believe I have the strength to go on." Tears streamed down his cheeks again.

Feeling compassion swell up inside of her, Darcy reached for his hand again. "Five days ago, I was lost, and I wasn't truly living my life. I was hiding from the demons of my past."

"What changed?" he asked softly.

Her bottom lip quivered as she revealed, "I met Porter. He saved me."

Adam lowered his head in defeat. "You love him," he murmured regretfully.

"With everything that I am." She waited till he looked up at her. "One day, a woman will be placed in your path and everything will become as it should be."

Wincing, he said, "Perhaps we don't mention to Porter that I proposed to you."

"I know why you did," she acknowledged, "and if circumstances were different, I might have accepted."

Adam released her hand and stood. "If you need anything, I will be back at the house."

Darcy nodded and watched as he walked out of the door. Taking a moment, she said a prayer for Adam. She had already walked his journey, and it was long and treacherous. How ironic that she had been assigned a case that allowed her unique, yet painful background, to provide comfort and relief to another.

Her heart longed to be near Porter. She quickly walked into the bedroom and sat down on the bed. Taking her hand, she brushed his hair from his forehead. "Please fight for me. I love you," she whispered.

Darcy moved his left arm and laid her head down on his beating heart. Till death do us part, she thought as she closed her eyes.

Porter felt like he'd been trampled by a horse. His whole body ached, but his right shoulder throbbed intensely. Then it came rushing back to him. He'd been shot.

His eyes jerked open at the thought of Darcy being in danger. What had become of her? He tried to sit up, but something held him down. That's when he noticed her safely tucked under his left arm, her head resting on his chest. He pulled her closer to him, immensely pleased that she was with him.

Darcy began to stir, and she turned her head to look up at him. Her eyes grew wide as she exclaimed, "You're awake!"

To his surprise, and horror, she burst into tears. "I have been so scared," she confessed through hiccups.

He grunted as he struggled to sit up and rest his back against the wall. "What happened?" he asked, wondering how to stop Darcy from crying. Why was she so emotional? She never cried. Suddenly, it dawned on him, and a feeling of pride washed over him. These tears were for him.

Darcy sat back and wiped the tears off her face. "After you jumped in front of me, and got shot," she paused, giving him a stern glare, "Adam and I both shot and killed Dustin. We rode as hard as we could until we brought you back here, so I could remove the bullet and stitch you up."

"It's over, then," Porter remarked. "We solved the case."

She nodded. "Adam was going to head up this morning to retrieve all the men's bodies from the cave. He insisted that they all have proper burials."

Porter winced as pain shot through his right shoulder. "How is Adam holding up?"

Darcy reached to the side of the bed and grabbed a bag off the table. She opened it and pulled out some bandages. "As well as can be expected," she shared. "We had a good talk last night while you were resting." She smiled to let him know that she was teasing.

"You two spent time alone last night?" he asked, attempting to keep his tone cordial.

She reached up and removed the bandaging from his wound. "Yes," she replied, her eyes focusing on his wound. "He even offered to let me stay on as his housekeeper."

"Did he now?" he grumbled.

As she rewrapped the wound, she replied, "With all the

newfound wealth he has, he offered me anything my heart desired."

Porter's body tensed, feeling an intense desire to shoot the man who'd hired them. "What did you say?"

She leaned back and smiled. "I told him that I already had what my heart desires."

"Which is?" he asked, hopefully.

"You," she confessed, placing her hand over his beating heart. "I love you."

He closed his eyes as he realized his gamble had paid off. He'd slowly courted her, peeling away each layer of grief and pain, one at a time. Now, she'd chosen him rather than living with the burdens of her past. His heart skipped a beat and only Darcy's frantic voice brought him back to the present.

"Porter? Did you hear what I just said?"

He opened his eyes slowly. "I am just trying to process the words."

"Oh," she replied, placing her bag on the table. "Let me go prepare you some breakfast."

Realizing that she had misconstrued his silence for hesitation, he grabbed her hand, forcing her to sit back down. "I never believed in love at first sight. But from the moment I met you, I knew that we were meant to be together." He brought her hand up to his lips. "I will fight for your love until my last breath, because you are the woman of my dreams."

Tears came to her eyes, but she blinked them away. "I love you, Porter Shaw."

"And I love you, Mrs. Shaw." A mischievous smile came to his lips. "If I recall at our first meeting, I believe I told you that you would be begging to kiss me by the end of the assignment."

Her lips curved to one side as she leaned closer. When her lips hovered over his, he felt her intoxicating warm breath brushing against his lips as she said, "As a nurse, I advise patients that it is not wise to engage in physical activities before they are fully recovered." She started to lean back.

Porter laughed as he reached out and placed his hand on the back of her neck. "Fine. I concede." He gently pulled her closer. "I am the one begging to kiss you."

That, apparently, was the right thing to say because she closed the distance between them and pressed her soft lips against his. Slipping his arm around her waist, he yanked her towards him, ignoring the pain radiating in his shoulder. Her lips parted in surprise, and he took advantage by deepening the kiss.

Darcy ran her hands behind his head and threaded them through his hair. He broke the kiss and rested his forehead against hers. How he loved this woman and how he marveled that she loved him in return!

"That was… nice," she whispered.

"Nice?" he repeated in surprise. "That was far more than just 'nice' to my way of thinking."

She sighed. "I suppose we will have to keep practicing until we get better at it."

He chuckled. "That sounds like a perfect solution."

Leaning back, she moved her hand to cup his right cheek. "Thank you for saving me from Dustin, and from myself. You have shown me how a man is supposed to care for his wife. It is now my turn to take care of you, husband."

"We have the rest of our lives to take care of each other," he replied. "And I, for one, am looking forward to that very much."

A playful gleam came to Darcy's eyes. "I suppose one more kiss before I make breakfast wouldn't hurt."

"One kiss… one hundred kisses," he murmured, pressing his lips into hers. Now that Darcy was finally in his arms, nothing else mattered. Only she mattered. And he would prove to her how much he loved her every single day.

It was much, much later before Porter was served breakfast, but the wait was… worth it.

Epilogue

———

Six months later

Porter was holding Darcy's hand as they strolled down the main street of Loco Hills in the New Mexico Territory. His eyes scanned the boardwalk and noticed that men of all ages were gaping at them as they walked by. "Is there a reason why everyone is staring at us?" he asked, debating about drawing his weapon.

Darcy laughed as she waved at the gentlemen that were lined up to watch them. "No, they are just surprised that I returned home and am holding hands with you."

He furrowed his brow. "Why would that surprise them?"

"Do you remember how I told you that I received over a hundred marriage proposals?"

"I do."

"Well, the proposals came from these men," she hesitated, her eyes scanning the boardwalk, "most of them."

A wagon pulled up next to them and a dark-haired cowboy shouted down, "Looking for a ride?"

"No, thank you," Darcy replied coolly, keeping her gaze straight ahead. "We don't take rides from strangers."

The cowboy laughed and pulled the break on the wagon. In a quick motion, he jumped down from the bench and pulled Darcy into a tight embrace. "Welcome home," he said, picking her up and spinning her in a circle.

Porter cleared his throat. Now he was seriously considering pulling his weapon, but Darcy's laugh gave him pause.

The cowboy stepped back and tipped his Stetson at him. "It is nice to finally meet you, Porter."

Darcy smiled at him. "I would like to introduce you to my brother, Michael Spencer."

Porter extended his hand and shook Michael's as relief washed over him. "It is nice to meet you as well. I was worried you were one of her former suitors."

"You couldn't throw a rock in this town and not hit one of her admirers," Michael teased.

Darcy placed her hands on her hips. "You failed to mention that I did not encourage any of them."

"It's good to have you home," Michael said, putting his arm around Darcy's shoulders. "Are you staying long?"

"For a week," Porter answered.

Michael dropped his arm. "Anna has been going crazy since we first received your telegram." He lowered his voice. "Does Porter know what you did yet?"

Darcy shook her head as her eyes darted towards him. Interesting, he thought. His wife was keeping a secret from him.

Porter stepped closer to her and asked, "Are you keeping a secret from me, Agent Shaw?"

"A secret?" she repeated back, feigning shock. "I couldn't possibly keep a secret from the greatest Pinkerton agent of all time."

He laughed. "Flattery, really?" He placed his hands on her hips. "I approve," he said before kissing her firmly on the lips.

A collective cheer went around the town. Porter looked around and saw all the men were whooping and howling at their display of affection. Darcy tucked her face into his chest, and he grinned down at her.

Michael leaned closer. "Perhaps it might be best to finish," he smiled, "whatever this is back on the ranch."

"Good idea," Porter agreed as he assisted his wife up to sit on the wagon bench next to her brother.

As they drove towards the ranch, Michael shared one story after another about Darcy's antics before she went off to finishing school. Darcy would periodically interrupt and contest the validity of the story. It was clear that Darcy and Michael shared a close bond.

His heart started to mourn the loss of contact he had with his brothers. It had been more than eight years since he had last seen them. Perhaps he would make some inquiries and discover where they were working now.

Coming over a hill, Porter had his first good look at the Shadow Ridge Ranch outfit. Buildings were scattered around the yard and fenced green pastures went as far as his eyes could see. "Your ranch is enormous," he remarked in awe.

Darcy nudged his shoulder. "You seem to forget that half of this ranch belongs to *us*, husband."

He shifted in his seat. "I had no idea you were an heiress."

"Heiress." Darcy chuckled. "Far from it."

Michael adjusted the reins in his hand. "So, I take it that you didn't marry my sister for her money."

Porter leaned closer and kissed his wife's cheek. "I married her because she is the bravest woman that I've ever met."

"Or was it because you were assigned to marry me?" Darcy teased.

Michael smiled over at them. "I can't wait to hear this story, but first…" His words came to a stop when the wagon pulled into the yard. "Why don't you show him the new cowhands that we hired a month ago? I believe I saw them walk into the barn just now."

Darcy's eyes held a glimmer of mischief as she replied, "I think that is a fine idea."

Porter jumped down and reached back up to assist his wife. As he lowered her to the ground, Darcy went back up on her tiptoes and kissed him. "Come," she said, grabbing his hand.

"Is it a tradition on your ranch to meet all the new cowhands?" Porter asked curiously.

"Oh, yes," she replied, smiling.

The barn door was wide open as they walked in. Two men were brushing down the horses, their backs towards them.

"Gentlemen," Darcy announced. "We are so excited that you are here with us."

The two men put down their brushes and turned around. Porter's eyes grew wide when he recognized his brothers. "Ben? Shawn?"

Ben, his older brother, smiled widely. "It's good to see you."

The next few moments were filled with hugs and much back-slapping. "I can't believe you're here," Porter murmured in awe. "How is this possible?" Except for a few wrinkles on their weathered faces, his brothers were exactly as he remembered them.

"Ask your wife," Shawn replied. "She offered us a large sum of money to come work at this ranch." He smirked as he corrected, "I guess it's your ranch as well."

Porter turned his grateful but puzzled gaze towards his wife. "How did you manage this feat?"

Darcy's eyes held unshed tears. "Our ranch always needs experienced cowhands."

"How did you even find my brothers?" he asked, approaching her.

"I asked Archie to make a couple of inquiries." She pressed her lips together. "Did I displease you?"

Porter stopped in front of her and reached for her hands. "Nothing you ever do could displease me. I can't believe you did this for me."

"I would do anything for you," she responded, her eyes full of love.

"I love you," he murmured before he kissed her. "One day you are going to realize that I don't deserve you."

"Never." She stepped back but kept hold of his right hand. "I have another surprise for you."

"There's more?" He turned back towards his brothers, and they just shrugged. As they walked towards the main house, Porter asked, "Are you happy?"

"So much that I feel my heart might burst," she answered.

"You have caught counterfeiters, murderers, embezzlers," he listed, "and that was only in your first six months of being an agent. Imagine what cases we will be assigned in the next six months."

"I can't wait." She stopped and turned to face him. "But I have a different adventure in mind after that."

He grinned. "Would you prefer to go after bank robbers?"

"Sounds delightful, but after that…" She took his hand and placed it over her stomach. "What about a baby?"

His eyes widened as his gaze lowered to her stomach. "Are you sure… I mean…?" he stammered out.

With a bright smile on her lips, she bobbed her head up and down. "The doctor confirmed it before we left."

He pulled her into a tight embrace and let out a whoop of joy as he twirled her in a circle. When he placed her down, he asked in a concerned voice, "Did I hurt you or the baby?"

"You could never hurt me," Darcy said.

Tears came to his eyes as he cupped his wife's cheeks. "You have made me the happiest man in the whole world."

She placed her hands over his. "Now you know how you make me feel every single day."

A bell started ringing from the main house, drawing his

attention towards the porch. "I take it that's the dinner bell?"

"It is." She stepped back. "Let's go share the good news with my brother and his wife."

Porter offered his arm as they strolled back towards the house. He couldn't believe how drastically his life changed the day he married Darcy. Every day he was with her was a blessing. He loved her more than he ever thought it was possible, and she showered affection and love on him without restraint. Together, they had become two of the best agents that the Denver office had to offer.

Whatever he'd done in his life that led up to finding Darcy, he must have done it right. He was a better man and a better agent with his wife by his side. And with a baby on the way, their adventures had only just begun.

The End

About the Author

Laura Beers spent most of her childhood with a nose stuck in a book, dreaming of becoming an author. She attended Brigham Young University, eventually earning a Bachelor of Science degree in Construction Management.

Many years later, and with loving encouragement from her family, Laura decided to start writing again. Besides being a full-time homemaker to her three kids, she loves waterskiing, hiking, and drinking Dr. Pepper. Currently, Laura Beers resides in South Carolina.

You can reach her at authorlaurabeers@gmail.com

CPSIA information can be obtained
at www.ICGtesting.com
Printed in the USA
LVHW090550120319
610337LV00001B/102/P